# A SINGLE STONE

# STONE

## MEG McKINLAY

**CANDLEWICK PRESS**

Copyright © 2015 by Meg McKinlay

First U.S. edition 2017

Library of Congress Catalog Card Number pending
ISBN 978-0-7636-8837-0

16 17 18 19 20 21 BVG 10 9 8 7 6 5 4 3 2 1

Printed in Berryville, VA, U.S.A.

This book was typeset in Mrs. Eaves.

Candlewick Press
99 Dover Street
Somerville, Massachusetts 02144

visit us at www.candlewick.com

For my mother and my daughter,
for all the things we share

# CHAPTER 1

*First the fingertips and then the hand. Choose your angle wisely, girl; there's no forgiveness in bone. Rotate the shoulder, let the head and hips follow . . . there.*

The Mothers' words echoed in Jena's mind as she eased into the crevice, flattening herself against the rock. When she was through, she paused, waiting for the next girl. They were deep now, in the heart of the mountain. Around her, the earth pressed so tightly it was hard to tell where her body ended and the stone began.

She sighed into the quiet dark. This was the work she loved—when there was nothing but ahead and behind, nothing but this steady movement on bellies and elbows. Seven girls nose to toe, wearing stone like skin as they made their way toward the harvest, a thin rope looping them together in an unbroken line. A finger extended, an elbow scythed onto rock, hunting leverage. A toe caught, kicked, gained for itself an inch. Another.

"Through there?" The voice was barely a whisper, but Jena heard the tremor in it all the same. The rope pulled at her waist as the girl behind her slowed and then stopped. "But how . . . ?"

"It's all right." Before Jena could reply, the answer came firmly from the back of the line. Though the voice had the hollow quality all sound took on down here, Jena knew immediately who it belonged to.

Kari might not have been chosen to lead the line, but there was no one more reliable. She was always ready with the right thing at the right time: a soft tug on the rope to remind a girl she was not alone, a handful of well-placed words to quell her rising doubt. "You'll be fine. You've trained for this. Just take it slowly."

"Of course. I'm sorry."

The rope slackened as the girl began to move, gingerly at first and then with more confidence. Jena waited until she was almost through, then resumed her own methodical progress, slowing every so often to press a hand to the rock or shine her head lamp into a fissure. Always searching, always probing. This way, or that?

The girl behind her did not speak again, but a few minutes later something brushed Jena's foot. The lightest finger-touch, a whisper all its own.

Jena would not fault the girl for it. She was young and Jena remembered those days herself—that urge to reach out, to feel, just for a moment, the warmth of flesh instead of stone.

What was this one's name again? As Jena twisted herself around a bend, her mind reached for it, then shied away. The village was not so large that a name would evade her if she truly wished to recall it. But it didn't matter yet. Not when a girl was so new, on her very first harvest. Not until you were sure she would last.

This girl was not the first they had trialed since the Mothers pulled Petria from the line, but she was by far the most promising. The last one had been a disaster; when the mountain began to narrow around her, she panted and flailed, hands thrashing at the rock.

There was no telling with some—the wooden training maze and shallow surface tunnels did not always predict how a girl would fare deep in the mountain. And though there was disappointment when the years of training came to nothing, the village tried not to lay blame. Not everyone could be born to the work of the harvest. Not everyone could adapt, or be adapted.

They would send that girl to the fields, Jena thought. She would be useful in a dull sort of way—turning the soil over, searching for yams and roots. Jena shivered at the thought of the blade striking earth. There was no place for a digger inside the mountain.

What they sought in here—the precious flakes of mica that would warm the village through the long, snowbound winter—did not call for digging. When the harvest was ready, it peeled away cleanly at the slightest touch. The mountain saw their need, made them a gift of it.

The sole of Jena's foot prickled where the new girl had traced her tentative fingernail.

It was late in the season to be breaking in a tunneler, but with Petria gone, there was little choice; they could hardly go in with just six.

It was better that the girl came now. Better that they knew if she would join them next season. Or if they might need to look to another. There were decisions to be made. Winter was nearly upon them; already there was a telltale crispness in the air.

Jena's belt snagged briefly as she hauled herself across a jagged rock. What few supplies she carried—a knife, a pouch, a flask of water, some straps of dried meat—were bound tightly against her side, so close they might almost have been part of her.

Just ahead, the space appeared to widen a little. Her eyes strained into the gloom. This deep, her head lamp offered no more than a feeble glow. The other girls carried their own, but these would remain unlit until Jena found the harvest and they spread out to begin flaking mica from the rock's surface.

Although it was the mica's warmth that kept the village alive, its light was useful too. When the line tunneled, it was mica chips they used in their lamps; they would not waste them when those behind had no need to see, when all they had to do was follow.

Sometimes Jena wondered whether she needed it herself. Perhaps she might make her way just as surely without the light. In her mind's quiet eye, the network of caves and interconnecting passages—the crevices and cracks through which the mountain allowed them entry—shifted this way and that, an invisible map remaking itself with every piece of ground.

There were real maps back at the village, a patchwork of pages the Mothers insisted Jena add to after each harvest. Though she did as directed, she had no use for them herself; their simple, flat surfaces could hardly speak for what was inside the mountain. The maps in her mind were complex and beautiful, intersecting and flowing across one another like living, growing things, but there was no way of getting them onto the page.

These days, each harvest carried them into new territory. The surface mica was long depleted, the shallow tunnels stripped generations ago. It was said that in the first years after Rockfall, in the time of the Mothers' great-great-grandparents, the line could go in for an hour and return with full pouches. But even if those stories were true, those days were long past. Every harvest called for them to go deeper—and darker.

As if to underscore the thought, Jena's lamp flickered, then dimmed. She reached into her pouch for another chip. Soon the mica would wink out altogether, throwing them into utter blackness.

She removed the dying chip from its housing and struck the new one with her fingernail. It flared immediately into pale-blue light, sending ghostly shadows onto the walls. She pressed it into place and then slid the spent chip into a crack in the nearby stone. It was the simplest of gestures.

6

Another girl might have tucked the chip into her pouch, carried it back to the village. It would not have been odd to do so, for spent mica had many uses. It could be hammered flat, rolled into sheets of metal from which things like tins and cooking pans were made. Most of the mica they burned was turned eventually to such purposes, and that was as it should be. In the closed world of the valley, waste was a luxury they could not afford. But it felt different when they were tunneling. In here, it seemed right that she return it to the mountain.

She crawled farther, feeling the stone walls recede around her, the sense of a weight easing off her shoulders. She raised her head, throwing the anemic glow from her lamp into the space in front of her.

It was a junction, a curving of the passage: one path to take, the other to pass by. She moved slowly forward, probing.

*This one,* she told herself. The way the darkness deepened just ahead. The slight mustiness that clotted the nostrils. There was air moving down there. A shaft somewhere.

She leaned closer and smelled again, to be safe. To be sure—that it was air and not some fetid stench, a gas long trapped that might wrap itself around them, lull them into a dreamless sleep. The mountain might keep a girl that way. A harvest might fail.

She drew a shallow breath. Another. It was only air. There was nothing here to trouble them.

She reached forward and pressed a hand to the ground. Odd. There was something loose there. Not a stone—this was longer, thinner. And now another.

*Oh.* Something in her drew back, clenched. A jolt of recognition coursed through her. The smoothness of bone beneath her fingers. Her hand closed around the brittle fragments even as her mind began to race, imagining.

An old rockfall? There was no sign of it.

She knew where her thoughts were headed and tried to reel them in. There was nothing to be gained from wondering about this girl—who she had been and how she had felt. That chilling moment when rope caught, when flesh wedged and would not budge. Did she struggle or give herself over to it, accepting what the mountain had decided?

Jena shook her head, bit down hard upon her lip. The bones rested light as leaves in her palm. There would be more, but she would not seek them. She would not feel around for the shape of the girl, for the coil of rope, its neatly sliced ends.

Nor would she tell the girls behind her. Because although the other passage was wide and this one the barest sliver, instinct told her it was the way. And if they were to pass through, they must believe they could. The smallest seed of doubt could grow so easily, split a girl open. Jena would not plant it.

She inhaled a long draft of the musty air, steadying herself. These bones were surely old. It was years since the village had given the mountain reason to keep a tunneler. These days, the girls who made up the line were leaner; years of painstaking management had seen to that. And they were more careful too, being sure to show respect to the mountain. They went in with seven and followed only those spaces the mountain had made for itself — fissures and crevices carved by water and time, caverns hollowed out naturally like the chambers of a heart. If they happened upon one of the tunnels their ancestors had gouged through the rock, they turned away, found another path. Each generation since Rockfall had learned more about what it took to survive — in the mountain and the valley both.

Jena probed the opening with her free hand. It was tight but passable.

She turned her feeble light to the wall. This was the way. There were always signs, if you cared to read them.

There was no need for her to say it; she had only to begin to move. The others would take the path she set, unseeing, trusting.

As she twisted through the opening, she allowed herself to hope. They had been four days without a harvest, returning to the village with empty pouches. But surely today would be different? The signs were stronger now, the stain spreading through the rock like sinew. Soon enough it would appear—the soft blue glow with which the earth revealed its secrets. She would come to a stop and press her back against the stone, letting the others fall in beside her.

They would strike their lights, bring forth their blades, perform their slow, methodical work. Perhaps they would rest awhile—eat a mouthful of leathery meat, take a drink from their flasks. Then offer their murmurs of gratitude and turn for home. To the village that nestled, like all else in the valley, in the mountain's vast shadow. As they approached through the fields, people would rise to greet them, eager for news. Glances would fall upon their pouches, hopeful, expectant.

But none would ask. It was to the Mothers that

Jena would deliver the harvest. To the dark room in the back of the Stores where it would be weighed and measured into rough hemp bags. Mother Berta would make her spidery notes in the ledgers, thin fingers running down one column after another. This much for a baker, that much for a carpenter; two scoops for this family, one for the next. To each according to their service—and their worth.

The thought was a comfort. That quiet room. A bountiful harvest. Berta at her desk in the pale-blue light, approval shining in her eyes.

*If the rock allows it.*

The words echoed in Jena's mind, natural as breathing. It was the mountain that would decide. In this, as in all things.

The bones sat smooth and cool in her palm. Her fingers curled around them as if they were a treasure, something she might keep—or take back to the village and sink in the graveyard beside her many sisters.

No. She let her fingers fall back like a flower opening. Whoever it was, let her rest here. Was it not, for a tunneler, a fitting place to lie—folded into the mountain, her bones crumbling eventually to become one with the stone?

In the dim light, Jena watched her shadow flash

across the rock. She set the bones to one side, then eased her way through the narrowing hole.

❋

Somewhere secret, Lia has her back to stone.

It is a secret because she should not be inside the mountain. It is a secret from Father and Mother and from everyone else too. No one is supposed to come here, but she cannot resist. Not since the very moment she found this place. What was it that made her look up that day? The shadow of a bird? Some unexpected shift in the light?

It is years ago now. She doesn't remember. What she does recall is the sudden thrill of surprise. It was almost nothing, and that was the charm of it. A sliver in the rock face, nearly—but not quite—concealed behind bushes. It was so unlike the other gaping wounds in the mountain's side, the great caverns people had hollowed out all those years ago.

Those are the spaces Father has told her to avoid, and she does so gladly. There is a violence to them, a wrongness—the jagged rock like torn flesh that has solidified.

But this place is different. It is like a slot that has

opened to receive her. The stone walls fit snugly around her, in a kind of embrace.

This is a way in, just for her. Even if she were not forbidden to come here, she would not tell anyone. The other girls are friendly enough, but they are different somehow. They are not the kind of girls who want to explore and find out, who want to follow paths and passages and ideas to their distant ends. If Lia showed them this place, they would wrinkle their noses and say she was strange.

Nothing about this feels wrong or strange. If there is anything odd, it is that it feels familiar—a return to a place Lia has never been. After the first time she came in, her limbs buzzed for days with something she could not explain.

She has been here many times since, has sat for hours inside the stony walls, has clambered and crawled through their endless forbidden crevices. Sometimes a flash of bluestone catches her eye and she turns her lamp's flame to the wall, trailing her fingers across the flaking surface. People split the mountain open for this once, but there is no need for that now. The plain that sweeps down to the sea is studded with it. It lies in rich, open veins right there on the ground.

Lia smiles at the thought. She reaches for the

bracelet at her wrist and rubs the smooth blue bauble between her fingers. It is the first present Father and Mother ever gave her; she will never take it off.

She sighs as she leans against the curve of the stone. People say the mountain is dangerous, that the stone is unstable and can move without warning. It did so once, many grandfathers ago, exploding and collapsing in a calamity of tumbling rock. Though none among Lia's ancestors saw it, the aftermath was clear enough. When they landed upon the shore, they saw the fresh scars upon the land, the gaping holes scoring the earth. And they knew that the wall of water that had taken their own tiny island, sweeping them into fragile boats on the wild sea, had visited here too.

But it was land, at least. This place was bigger, and the waters had drawn back, leaving it high and dry, livable. Their home was gone, but here was somewhere to begin again.

Lia cannot imagine the mountain behaving in such a way. It is not, she thinks, in its nature. The stone walls around her feel solid, an immovable mass, unbreachable by any force she can conjure in her imaginings.

She sets one hand upon the rock. It is cold and warm all at once. It is solid. It is always.

*You mustn't go there,* people say. *It is treacherous.*

And yet it feels nothing like that. It feels like opening the door on a winter night, stepping across the threshold to a waiting hearth.

It feels like coming home.

# CHAPTER 2

First there was light. The darkness eddied around Jena, then receded.

There was sky up ahead, the faintest smudge of blue. A wisp of white drifted past. Cloud. Autumn breeze. The promise of outside.

She crawled toward it. Because they had a harvest and this was what came next. *Make the harvest. Find the light.*

It was close now, the tunnel sloping upward as it approached the opening in the mountain's flank through which they had entered shortly after dawn. Where stone ended and sky began, there was a narrow lip, a ledge that sat between the two like a shelf. There was headroom here, and more. Jena loosened the knot at her belt and then patted herself down, sweeping small stones and dirt from her hair and clothes. Perhaps it was silly, but it felt like something, a gesture—to do what you could, to leave what belonged here to the mountain. A trade, of sorts, for what they had been given.

When she had finished, she squeezed her eyes tightly shut. This too was a habit she had acquired over the years—closing her eyes as she emerged so she would be out suddenly rather than gradually. So it felt less like a choice and more like something already done, to which she must simply adapt. She felt her way forward and brought her legs around, swinging them over the rim of the ledge.

When she opened her eyes, the sheer walls towered above and all around. She was at a slight overhang; a few feet below the lip of the rock, the mountain sloped down into the clotting dark of the forest.

Even as Jena had led the others up here this morning, she had known they would have to be careful going back down. The slope was steep and the surface was an unsteady scree of rounded stones, any one of which could easily turn an ankle. She moved forward a little farther. Her legs swung freely at first, dangling out into space. Then she hooked her knees over the ledge and shuffled to the side, making room for the girl behind.

"Oh! You can see everything."

*Min.* The name came to Jena as if something had clicked into place inside her head. *A first daughter,* Mother Berta had said. A first daughter, but a sixth child. Jena winced, thinking of the hunger, the cold. The weight of a whole family on those fragile shoulders.

Min edged into the opening, craning to see. It had barely been light when they entered, and in any case a girl on her first harvest would have had more important things on her mind than the view.

She squinted in the light, swiveling left, then right. "It's so different from up here."

Jena followed Min's gaze across the treetops. The whole world was laid out before them. On the far side, the village nestled in a sheltered corner, bordered by rock wall in the north, the fields to the east, and the spreading forest in the south and west. And all of that by the towering ridges of the mountain, the strong stony fingers that encircled the valley, cupping the land in the palms of its hands.

It must have been around midday, for there was a wide shaft of sun upon the valley. With the season drawing to a close, there was hardly any heat in it, but the light alone was almost warming. The mountain's soaring peaks meant the valley had only a few hours of full sunlight each day; each beam felt precious, worth savoring.

There was little movement below, with most of the village and its fields shrouded by the surrounding trees. The tops of the tallest buildings were visible, along with the spindly ventilation pipes that protruded from each house. When the winter snows fell, these would allow them fresh air, at least for a time. They put Jena in mind of the reeds that clustered along the banks of the spring; she couldn't help imagining creatures hidden below the water, mouths pressed hopefully to the ends.

Although the valley looked peaceful from here, the old wounds were still there. Remnants of the time they called Rockfall were everywhere, ugly outcrops of stone dotting the ground like tumors. There was no way to repair such assaults on the earth—the ground had split itself open as if it were being carved by an invisible knife. These things could not be undone, but the passage of time had softened the transgressions of the past: the deep-green moss coating the low ridges that radiated through the forest from the base of the mountain, the tangle of ivy covering the massive boulders that had shaken loose all those years ago. From here, you could set history aside and see it as nothing but beautiful.

That was, if you didn't turn toward the Gash, the jagged wound in the mountain's side where everything had ended. Everyone knew the story of Rockfall. It was a tale that had shaped their lives, whose aftermath they lived every day.

Before Rockfall, their world had been outside. People lived on the plain that sloped away from the mountain, a narrow band of undulating land that lay between it and the edge of the island. Back then, the valley was just a place people came to from elsewhere. Though the ring of mountains formed an almost-closed circle, there had been a way through, a single point where the stony hands tapered down to form a natural passage. Every day, people walked through the place they called the Pass, coming here to pick herbs and berries or trap the landbirds that favored the shelter of the forest. Or to spread out a blanket and eat lunch in the shade by the spring that bubbled up from the valley floor.

People did other things here too, things that seemed beyond imagining now. Men worked side by side to split open the mountain. They blasted holes big enough to stand in, then swarmed inside with shovels and pickaxes. They hacked at the rock, taking whatever they wanted—some things simply because they were shiny or pleasing to the eye. The mountain's deepest secrets were shaped into baubles and trinkets; the translucent blue of the mica dotted earlobes and hung in windows.

The Gash was not the only place their ancestors had wronged the mountain, but it was where the rock fought back. Where it finally said *enough.* It opened its throat and swallowed their world, and them with it. Of those digging, only a handful survived. And did so only to find themselves trapped, along with everyone else who had come to the valley that day. When the rocks finally stopped falling, the Pass had closed; what had been sheer walls on either side were collapsed upon each other in a tight jumble of stone. Those in the valley were encircled by rock, utterly enclosed, the mountain soaring above and around them, its treasures sealed deep once more, beyond reach.

Mother Berta's grandson, Luka, said she had a necklace with a mica pendant, a teardrop of luminous blue stone that had been passed down to her. That she kept it in a chest, snug between layers of heavy fabric.

Jena had scoffed when he told her. When the snow grew too deep for chimneys and hopeful reeds, mica was the only fuel the village could safely burn. It was the difference between life and death, and there was little enough to spare. None among them would hoard a trinket while others froze.

A shiver ran through her. How terrible that first winter must have been. The Rockfall survivors could not have anticipated how deep the snow would fall—that the mountain's peaks would act as a funnel, the small valley as a basin, building it up and up, above and around them, the stone walls that ringed their world seeming to intensify the cold. That their choice, snowbound inside their huts, would be between starvation, freezing, or suffocation.

With their chimneys buried in snow, the smoke from the wood fires had nowhere to go but back inside. There was no way to warm themselves and no way to cook. There was no way to get out and no way to remain.

When spring finally came, they had lost several of their number. The elderly, the weak. When they had dug their way out through the softening snow, they began to dig graves.

Over the years, they learned. They found ways to manage better. The ventilation pipes, which bought them time. But most of all the mica, which burned cleanly, leaving nothing in its wake. No smoke or fine particles that would steal your breath and choke you from the inside. When mica was spent, it simply blinked out.

Jena patted the bulging pouch she had lashed against her belt. It was a good harvest. She had been right about the signs.

"Come on, Jena!" Loren called from the middle of the line. Her voice was lighthearted but betrayed a note of impatience.

"Just a minute!" Jena motioned to Min to loosen the rope that looped through her belt. The other girls would follow in turn, working the knots until they yielded. The rope was made of tightly woven ragvine and was thin but tough, almost wiry. Inside the mountain, they wore it doubled over, giving them extra length in case they needed it for a long descent. When they were tunneling, it bound the line together, but once the knots were undone, it slipped easily away.

"Come on," Jena said to Min. She pushed lightly off the ledge and onto the ground below, stiffening as her feet sent a flurry of stones skittering across the slope. Then she checked herself. They were just rollers, surface-dwellers the mountain had shed like dead skin. No one would fault her for that.

She watched Min push herself clear. The girl slid almost soundlessly out and down, her hands extended just enough for balance. When her feet found ground, she stood there, contained, as if the rock were still around her, as if she were unsure how to handle the sudden rush of space.

Jena allowed herself the flicker of a smile. It was seven years since her own first harvest, but she remembered that feeling, the odd sensation of her limbs suddenly moving unchecked into the outside. This was as sure a test as any, she had always thought. What came naturally here said more somehow than the years of training.

This girl would do well and that was a relief.

The others had emerged, and now Kari was out, letting the momentum of her descent carry her down the slope. She skidded to a stop, feet shoveling through the loose stones, and grinned when she saw Jena frown.

"They're rollers, Jena. Stop worrying."

"I'm not."

"Of course you are." Kari put an arm around her. "You always worry. I bet you did that eye-closing thing too."

Jena flushed. She hadn't meant to share her funny

little rituals with Kari; it had just happened somehow, a natural consequence, perhaps, of all the nights they spent at arm's length from each other, snug in the tiny room that had only been meant for one.

"You did, didn't you?" Kari laughed and reached back to loosen her braid. She combed her fingers roughly through her hair, working from the bottom up. When they were inside, the girls all wore their hair in this style, pulled back from their faces and woven tightly. It was practical for tunneling, but there was more to it than that; it simply felt wrong to leave something loose that might be contained. It was for this reason too that even though their years of wrapping were long past, they still bound their hips and chests when they tunneled, as if to say, *We are doing what we can.*

Jena glanced down the slope at Min. She had hurried to a nearby bush and was crouched behind it.

Kari's eyes sparkled with amusement. "They always drink too much the first time." She turned toward Jena, her expression thoughtful. "She did well, didn't she? She'll be good."

"Yes, I think so."

"Calla said she was a cleanskin."

Jena's gaze took in Min's slender frame, resting briefly on her hips, then shoulders. Through her thin cotton garments, she could see the outline of jutting bone.

There was something right and natural about a girl like that. It sometimes seemed to Jena that those who had been adjusted had a stunted quality, as if they had been reduced from a larger version of themselves. Some said such girls did not take to the line as easily as cleanskins, but if that were true, Jena had seen no evidence of it.

In the mountain, in the dark, it didn't matter what you looked like. It didn't matter whether you had been born into your smallness or helped along by the knife, by the careful breaking and compression of your bones. It mattered only that you could get the work done.

A few feet farther along, Renae sat with Asha, their eyes fixed in the direction of the village. Thinking of home, Jena supposed. Of a soft bed and a handful of something to ease the ache in their stomachs.

As much as it was what every girl dreamed of, tunneling was hard work. It sapped them of their reserves, and they had little enough of those. Jena too could feel hunger hollowing her out.

But as eager as they might be to head for home

and food, it was important that they wait. That they take some time to stretch a tentative arm, massage the cramping knots from a leg. That when they stood, they did so slowly, so the sky didn't rush to their heads, making them dizzy. Making them fall.

Jena had seen it happen in her first season. Had watched a girl waver where she stood, like a flame about to go out in the wind.

*I should have run,* she thought later. If she had, she might have reached the girl before she crumpled — limbs folding onto themselves, knees buckling beneath her. But Jena had been young then, and new; she hadn't known what was coming. For months afterward, the sickening crunch had replayed itself in her mind.

A fall was bad enough. But fainting was so much worse. A girl unconscious had no chance of remembering what the Mothers drummed into them over years of training: *Do not fall. But if you must fall, make yourself limp. Be like water. Be soft upon the ground.*

The girl had hit so hard.

That awful sound. Something shattering. The white gleam of bone breaking the surface.

A break was nothing like an adjustment. There was no planning in it, no control. An adjustment could advance a girl; a break could be the end of her days in the mountain.

Jena turned to Kari. "We'll wait awhile."

"Of course."

Jena felt a flush of gratitude. She knew Kari was eager to get back, to see her mama, to place a hand on her belly and wait for the fluttering movements that had lately begun to ripple her skin. They both were. But their work was not done until the harvest was secured and the line safely home, and this was something Kari would not question. She would wait and keep a watchful eye on the others until Jena said it was time to move on.

Jena raised herself onto the tips of her toes and peered out toward the village, resting an arm on Kari's shoulder. It would take them over an hour to get back, perhaps two. Although you were never far from anything else in the valley, the paths through the forest were not direct. They looped around themselves, following the flattest ground they could between the rugged outcrops of stone.

Jena had begun to lower her eyes to the slope and choose a place to sit when something caught her eye. Through the air above the village a thin column of smoke was rising. It was faint enough that you might easily miss it in the shifting light. And yet clear enough that once you had seen it, there was no question it was there.

She stared uneasily across the valley. There might be smoke in the Square, she told herself. The bakery, stoking its ovens. The smokehouse, where people would be preparing birds and rabbit for the winter stores. Or perhaps one of the kilns, where rollers and water stones were melted and shaped into metal and glass. Like everything else, wood was carefully rationed, but daytime fires might burn for such purposes, for the good of all.

But this was not that kind of smoke. There was a puff of color, a greenish tinge Jena had seen from only one kind of fire. And it was not coming from the Square. It was fainter over the center of the village, as if it had drifted there on the breeze, thinning out on its way from somewhere else. She tracked its passage backward, to where it was thicker. And as she did, the skin on her arms pimpled into gooseflesh.

East. The edge of the village.

But it was too early for that. Much too early.

Her arm stiffened on Kari's shoulder. She turned and saw the flash of realization, alarm flooding Kari's face.

A sick feeling roiled deep in Jena's stomach, and with it a surge of recognition—that instant when you had to look squarely at something that changed everything.

The smoke. Its color. Its origin.

East, where the houses in the very back of the village nestled by the curving wall of the mountain.

Kari's house. Their house.

"No," Kari rasped.

Her arm wrenched abruptly from Jena's shoulders. "I have to go. I . . ."

And then she was gone, tiny stones scattering behind her as she careered headlong down the slope.

# CHAPTER 3

The forest blurred around Jena. Thin branches
whipped across her skin. A footfall ahead, Kari was
sprinting, arms pumping by her sides, hands clawing
at the air as if to pull herself forward. When Kari
took off, Jena had recoiled at the way she flailed,
legs tangling, arms windmilling as she tried to find
speed.

Then she had followed, stumbling behind Kari
down the slope.

Wouldn't she run too, if it were her own mama?

Hadn't she, when it was?

Kari's cheeks were flushed and her mouth was
open, panting. Her straw-blond hair, kinked into
ridges from the braid, streamed behind her. Every
now and then a strand caught roughly on a twig before

being yanked clear; Jena was glad to have left her own hair tightly bound.

Their feet pounded the forest floor, their cadence coming together for a time, then separating again. The pattern repeating, over and over.

Branch, rock, mossy log. There was no time for the eye to rest on anything. There was only foot over foot, leaping and turning. Jena's chest pounded, protesting this sudden exertion after the hours of slow, deliberate movement.

"You . . . okay?" Kari's breath came in short, rasping snatches.

Their eyes met briefly and Jena read the fear etched in Kari's. "Nearly there." The steadiness in her own voice came as a surprise.

In reply, Kari surged forward, drawing ahead along the widening path. Her shirt had come loose and fluttered at her side like the wing of a wounded bird. The morning's tunneling had loosened her wrappings, and where the skin was exposed, Jena saw flashes of red—patches of flesh that had been scraped and torn. Each trip laid new wounds over those that had barely healed from the last, each girl's body becoming its own kind of map.

In the middle of this, scoring Kari's lower back

near her right hip, was a crosshatch of translucent marks, the skin there so white it looked as if it had been polished. Though Kari's had only been a small adjustment, she would carry these scars always. You didn't cut into flesh—and bone—without leaving something behind.

As if in sympathy, Jena felt a sudden white-hot strobing in her own back—high up, between her shoulder blades. Though she had never been adjusted, she was not without her own scars.

Something like a sob choked from Kari's throat. "It was green, Jena."

"I know."

"Do you think it's her? It can't be, can it?"

Jena knew Kari wasn't really seeking an answer. Green smoke meant one thing only. It meant a man stumbling through the dusty streets, sentences barely formed, stammering alarm. A Mother hurrying from the Stores with a slim-necked bottle in her hand. To a house where a woman bit hard upon her lip, setting herself against whatever was to come. It meant willow-wort bubbling on the stove. The sleeves of a Mother's cloak flapping as she fanned the flames. Anxious glances down the hall.

Boiled to its essence, willow-wort was the strongest

painkiller they had. At its most potent when freshly distilled, it was used mostly as a birthing tonic. In addition to boiling it, the Mothers would place some directly upon the fire so it would infuse the very air around them. It was this that gave the smoke its greenish hue. It was this that made Jena's heart catch in her throat.

"But she's only six moons. It's too early."

Jena would have reached a hand to Kari if it would not have risked unbalancing them both. She understood only too well the fear that gripped her.

Early was good in a certain way of looking, if the baby was a daughter, which was of course what they hoped. Early meant small. It meant docile and sleepy, a baby who was content to give herself to the long days of stillness and compression that were to come. Who might one day follow her sisters into the network of narrow tunnels that was their birthright.

It meant all of that, if the child survived. But there was such a thin veil between *early* and *too early*. Six moons was on the very edge of things. A six-moon baby might hover between this world and the next, take a single rattling breath and slip quietly away.

If things went badly, it might take its mama too. People said smaller babies were easier on the mamas, and that seemed to be true when they were eight moons or nine. But when a baby was born so early, it was as if the mama's body was caught too much by surprise, everything coming hard and fast and wrong. An early daughter could be the hope of the future, but it could also be the death of it.

As quickly as the thought fluttered across her mind, Jena batted it away. "Nearly there."

This time it was almost true. They had entered the last sweeping bend before the path came out of the forest and into the flat sameness of the fields. The curve hauled them along its smooth arc like the weight on a pendulum. The silver flash of the spring. The final stand of trees, the forest thinning in carefully managed patches where men had been felling for the winter stores. Into the sun as they reached the fields with their patchwork of crops aligned in neat rows — what little they were able to grow in the windows of light the mountain allowed them. Potatoes. Carrots. Beets. All of it ready for the Wintering harvest.

The village, the streets that radiated from the Square like the spokes on a wheel.

The next corner and the next. Left. Right. Toward the dark arch of the mountain at the village's far perimeter. Down the narrow lane that led to the row of houses that sat in the lee of the mountain, in shadow.

East, to Kari's house.

*Our house,* Jena corrected herself. *Home.*

Strange how her thoughts went back to the old place in unguarded moments, the years between unstitching themselves like a loose-knit garment.

She shook her head. Those were the years that had mattered. The years that had made her.

She had pulled ahead without meaning to, and now she shortened her stride, letting Kari draw alongside. They were so close now. Soon it would be over. A new life would be held aloft, or it wouldn't. In the days to come, the Mothers might call them to a burial, perhaps two. It was the way of things; that was all. No reason, then, for this mad headlong dash, this urgent scramble homeward.

Unless it was to say good-bye. If there was nothing to be done, that at least was something.

The last corner now. The final turn.

They took it together and then stopped.

# CHAPTER 4

The street teemed with people. At the far end, the house was almost completely obscured behind the crowd. The village had gathered the way it might for a handful of occasions. A feast. A birth. A funeral.

Kari gripped Jena's arm, fingernails etching half-moons into her skin.

There was an acrid smell in the air, unmistakable. But the smoke itself was hard to make out. It had been clearer from the fields. And clearest of all from the slope, at the greatest of distances. It was possible, after all, to be too close to a thing. By standing in the center of it, to make it invisible.

Kari's hand tightened. The crowd parted, peeling back to let them pass. Familiar faces swam in and out of focus—Asha's older sister, Erin, who worked in the fields, her face red and prickled with sweat; Calla's brother, Ralf, his woodcutting arms thick with knobbed muscle. Behind him, a familiar dark head bobbed up and down. It was Luka, his slight frame almost comical alongside the older boy's. He joggled on his toes, craning to see. His eyes locked briefly on Jena's, and an instant was all she needed to read everything written there. Hope. Fear.

She kept moving. Around them, voices murmured. *A daughter is coming. It will be a day. If the rock allows it.*

A small figure stepped in front of them, halting their passage. Mother Vera's eyes contracted to fine points. "Child, do you have a harvest?"

"Yes," Jena said quickly. "We—"

"Where is it?"

Jena's hand went instinctively to her front. Usually, she gathered the pouches from the others and hung them across her chest from the rope, the way a hunter might wear the pelts of his quarry. There was a sharp stab of panic before she remembered.

"I didn't think." She gestured at the house. "We saw the smoke. I . . ."

Vera pursed her lips briefly. "All right." Her eyes dropped to Jena's belt, appraising. "Seven times what you carry?"

"More or less."

"A good harvest, then. Thanks be." She turned toward the house. "And a new daughter. It will be a day."

"If the rock allows it." Jena's response came easily, without thought.

"Just so." Vera stepped aside to let them pass.

The crowd funneled them forward. Ahead, the house squatted low, waiting. Behind it, the mountain curved, tall and dark. All of it was cast into sharp relief, like something seen for the first time. It was as if the world had narrowed to this alone.

The yard now, the stubby timbers of the veranda. The rough sod and thatching on the roof, the ragged hide stretched across the shuttered windows. Jena let Kari draw her along, her own hands leaden with the numbness of a dream. But when they reached the doorway, she stopped.

"Jena?"

Her eyes met Kari's. She gave a small shake of her head. For so long, this had been the only home she knew. But it was not hers today, not for this.

After a long beat, Kari nodded. She stepped through the doorway and was gone, swallowed by the shadows inside.

The door swung closed behind her, but Jena didn't need to see to know what was in there. The darkened hall, the low-roofed room at the end, the Mothers gathered, waiting, urging.

It had been ten years since her own long walk down the corridor.

*But not this one,* she reminded herself. Her gaze flicked to the space where her house had been. It was a relief now that it was gone, now that it no longer stood there like a decaying skeleton, its timbers half-stripped like flesh hanging from bones. It made it easier to forget, to let the past be the past. To let her old family fall away behind her, as she knew they must.

"It's good you came."

Jena turned to see Renae's mama, her hair flour-flecked and tangled from the bakery. She had never been a tunneler; her body was tall and thickset, her limbs heavy. The arm that gripped Jena's shoulder was solid and muscled from kneading dough.

"It will be all right, child."

At the woman's touch, something lurched inside Jena. The crowd was so loud, the crisp autumn air suddenly stuffy and close. The world became a wall of bodies pressing toward the house, toward her.

Something had shifted; a kind of pressure was building, a moment stretched hard against its breaking point.

"I'm sorry. I . . ."

She shrugged the arm roughly away, then placed a hand on the doorknob and pushed against it. She would wait just inside, close the door tight behind her.

But as she stepped into the house, her knees buckled. A thick smell fugged the air in the hall, sickly sweet. She felt suddenly dizzy, as if something deep within her had come loose. The smell was inside her, clogging her nostrils, stoppering her throat. Her vision blurred, making the figures down the hall ripple and sway. A familiar face turned toward her, eyes wide with alarm.

And now the walls were a tunnel around her, a narrow band of dark, collapsing and dwindling to a single fine point. Carrying her down.

❋

*Jena is four, perhaps five.*

*They have told her to run, and so she is running.*

*She hurtles through the streets, not knowing why but everything in her alive with the thrill of it. Because she is special, unwrapped early. The Mothers did not come for the other girls, not even Kari who lay right beside her.*

*There was one pair of hands only, reaching down into the bed, lifting her out. Turning and unwinding until the last of her wrappings had fallen away and she was free.*

Straight home, *the Mother said.* Go, child.

*When she rounds the corner, the street is full of people, their faces shining. When they see her, they step aside.*

You have a sister, *someone says, and Jena thinks,* Oh. So that's what it is.

*She had known there was a sister coming. A baby, at least. Mama said it was a daughter, but the Mothers said you can never be sure. It doesn't do to wish too hard. Only to wait and hope.*

It is the mountain that will decide.

In this, as in all things.

*The Mothers have taught Jena the words, and they roll smoothly from her tongue.*

*But it is strange that it is today. Mama's belly is big — so big it makes Jena laugh — but Papa says it isn't time yet, that the baby won't come until the first snow is high on the mountain.*

*Still, when Jena reaches the house, there she is, white and tiny, sneaking her birthday in early. A Mother stands on the doorstep, holding her up, smiling.*

*Jena wants to hold her too. She reaches for her and says,* Please, *because it is her sister and she has been waiting.*

42

*But the Mother shakes her head. She says,* Go, child, *and points down the hall.*

Mama.

*She looks pale and tired, but Jena knows that's how mamas are when a baby comes. They are weak for a while and have to stay in bed. The papas make soup, and you tell them it's delicious even though it tastes like water. Then each day the mamas are a little better, until before you know it they are up again, singing and smiling and taking the pot back, saying,* Here, let me.

*Jena knows this because Loren told her. Her mama has already had two babies after Loren, but they are both brothers. Loren will be jealous of Jena's tiny new sister.*

Mama. *Jena finds herself whispering because the room is so quiet. There is Papa and two Mothers and a strange kind of heaviness.*

Jena. *Mama's voice is soft, but that is okay because that's what mamas do sometimes. They come in the night when you wake up sad or frightened or sick. They speak gently and sing you back into dreaming.*

*There is something sweet on Mama's breath, and Jena's nose wrinkles. Sweet is good — it means some wickerberry for the porridge or honey for the bread. But this is neither of those things; this is on Mama and in the air around them. It is the smell of a birthing, she supposes. Or of a baby.*

43

*The word echoes in her mind, making her smile.*

*She will hold the baby later. She will ask Papa and he will let her. Even if it is only for a minute, before the Mothers take her to the Center. She will lower her face and breathe her in, the sweet, new smell of her.*

Look after your sister, *Mama says now, and she will.*

*Mama slips a hand from the bedclothes and reaches for Jena.*

Oh. *Her hand is damp beneath Jena's fingers. It is hot and cold all at once.*

Mama?

*The bedcover shifts, falls away.*

*There is a blanket underneath, and a white sheet. Only it is not white, because something is blooming across it like a strange flower — a stain of red spreading toward the edges of the bed.*

Mama? *Jena says again, her small voice unsteady.*

*Fingers flutter in her hand.* It's all right.

*But it isn't.*

*Later, they come for Mama. There is a special place, Papa says, where the Mothers will get her ready to go in the ground. Soon they will put her there. And Jena will go with Papa, with the village, to say good-bye.*

*She will remember then, Jena thinks — the fluttering fingers, the swift red flower. But she will not cry.*

Mama has had a good leaving, *she tells herself.* She has given us a daughter, a sister.

It is a day. *She repeats the words over and over. The Mothers have said so, and it must surely be. The rock has allowed it.*

*She will not cry. She will set her mouth in a line and take the stone from Berta's trembling hands. She will kneel and place it soft upon the quiet earth, and she will say good-bye.*

*For that is what a girl does when her mama goes.*

# CHAPTER 5

"Stand up, child."

There were arms under Jena, lifting, insistent, a fog of warm breath on her neck. The voice was unmistakable.

"Mother Berta." She set a hand against the wall, willing strength into her legs. "I—"

"You're all right."

Was it a question or a command? Jena turned to face her.

"You're all right," Berta repeated, and it was a statement now, a matter-of-fact quality to it that allowed for no other possibility. Her voice was hard-edged, but there was kindness in it too. Jena had spent enough time with her over the years to hear it.

"Were you dizzy? Kari said you ran back."

Jena hesitated. They had run and she was dizzy; that much was true. But she was not sure the two things were connected.

The smell lingered in the air, though it seemed to have eased. Perhaps it was something else on the fire — a medicinal herb or root used for the birthing — its strength ebbing and flowing with the force of the flames?

*Willow-wort for pain? Calumb for healing?* She called up the only names she could think of. But she was a tunneler, not a healer. It could be either of those or one of a hundred other things whose names she would never have reason to know. Whatever it was, it had reached back across the years, dragging her with it. She felt shaky still, as if the ground beneath her might shift without warning.

She turned to Berta. "That smell . . . ?"

Berta looked sharply at her. Then her expression softened and she placed a hand on Jena's arm. "You need air. Come."

As she steered Jena outside, there was a flurry behind them. One of the younger Mothers hurried from the kitchen, steam rising from a bowl in her hands. She disappeared into the bedroom at the end of the hall.

Another question formed on Jena's lips. "Do you know anything? Is she . . . ?"

"Not yet."

"It's so early. She—"

"I know, child." The reply was firm but gentle. "But we must trust."

Berta went to place a hand on Jena's shoulder but then let it fall back, as though the effort of reaching were almost too much for her. Berta had always been small and seemed to have become more so lately, as if a weight were settling upon her with the passing of the years. She had the birdlike frailty common to all who had tunneled—her back hunched, her shoulders stooped. Wiry, graying hair was pulled back around her weathered face into a tight bun. There was something filmy about her eyes, as if they had slipped behind a haze of cloud. But Jena knew there was little they didn't see.

They were outside now, and Berta closed the door with a click. A sigh rippled around them. The crowd had been waiting, Jena realized, for someone else to come through that door. They had been waiting for news.

"Mother Berta?" a voice called. Berta held up a hand.

The yard was full of people, but they had stopped at the line of the veranda. Jena was grateful, for it meant there was space—and air—around her. Then it came—somehow close and distant all at once—the faintest of cries, slicing the air like a fine-edged blade. A second followed almost immediately, this one stronger than the first.

The crowd fell silent. It was as if the village shared a single breath. Held it, waiting. Footsteps padded down the hall—no haste in their step, each footfall precisely measured, just so.

Jena moved aside as the door opened. Leathery arms grasped a tiny, naked bundle. Mother Elena stepped onto the veranda and the crowd drew back, all eyes fixed on the child.

Alive. That was the first thing.

A daughter. That was the second.

They knew this without being told, without searching the newborn's features for some telltale sign. If the child had been a boy, the Mothers would have emerged empty-handed. They would have filed quietly from the house, leaving the family to their disappointment.

A boy was simply another mouth to feed, another body to keep warm through the winter. A boy might wield an ax or trap a bird. He might mend a roof or skin a rabbit.

Such things were useful; there was no denying it. But a daughter? A daughter could do those too, and much more besides.

*If the rock allowed it.*

The crowd was waiting for the third thing.

The bundle looked small, but that was no kind of measure; didn't they all seem so in the arms of the Mothers?

Last year, the village had pinned its hopes on the butcher's baby. She had seemed slight and delicate, almost fragile. Jena had held her breath for the numbers, but when the Mother finally spoke, her voice was flat.

"Sixty-two. Fifty-nine."

The shoulders. The hips.

This was what mattered. This was the difference between the mountain and the fields.

Low fifties was a good-enough number; the Mothers could work with that if they must. But forties was better. Forties meant a girl who would take easily to the regimen, who might be molded and shaped without undue hardship or the need for extreme adjustments.

High fifties—*sixties?*—was another thing altogether;

there were some facts of nature for which nothing could compensate.

"Pfft." The miller's wife had spat on the ground and walked away. It was not long before others did the same.

That would not happen today, though. Kari was a tunneler, and Mama Dietz before her. This new daughter would surely follow.

*If the rock allows it.* The words echoed in Jena's mind as Mother Dyan came through the door with a measuring ribbon in her hands. Her fingers would be marking the numbers, holding the place where she had stretched the fabric tight. Dyan held up a hand, as if to quiet the already-silent gathering. She cleared her throat.

"Forty. Forty."

Jena waited. The Mother must have repeated the first number, making sure they had heard before moving on to the next.

But Dyan did not continue. She held the ribbon high, and there was just one finger on it, marking just one place.

*Forty and forty?*

"Thanks be," someone said — tentative and hesitant, as if they could not quite believe their own words.

Jena stood perfectly still. It was better than they had hoped for. Better than anyone could have dared imagine.

"Thanks be!"

"It is a day!"

Exclamations rose from the crowd. Faces creased in broad smiles. Cheers rang out and people jostled forward.

"Hold her up!" A voice rang out from the rear. "Let us see!"

Elena stepped into the light. She lifted the baby in a swift movement and held her aloft, the breadth of one hand almost encircling the tiny frame, the other placed loosely behind her head.

Immediately, the infant stiffened. She seemed to draw back into herself, then release, both arms flying out from her sides. She let out a gulping cry, arms flailing, feet swinging wildly in the air.

"Fool!" Berta strode past Jena. "Give her to me."

The younger Mother obeyed without a word. With one arm, Berta brought the baby in to her chest. With the other, she pulled the shawl from around her own shoulders. She began to wrap the baby, pulling the material swiftly from limb to limb until the swaddling was complete and the only skin visible was her face.

Jena felt herself exhale and realized she had been holding her breath, some part of her sharing the feeling of being suddenly untethered, cast adrift with nothing to hold on to.

The baby quieted immediately. A calm came over her, and her eyelids seemed to sink, heavy under their own weight.

What Berta had done was not real wrapping, but it was enough for now. It was what an infant craved after spending so many moons inside, curled tightly upon itself.

More Mothers emerged, filing down the hall and out onto the veranda. They cooed and clucked over the baby in Berta's arms. As Mother Anya, who had trained Jena in the maze, came past, she nodded back toward the house.

"All is well, child."

Jena felt weak with relief. The sweet smell had receded and something new was taking its place—richer and stronger. This was a smell Jena knew, as did everyone in the village—from childhood cuts and scrapes, from broken bones and stinging burns.

*Calumb for healing.*

There was a daughter, alive and tiny, a mama who would live to see her grow.

Jena stared through the door and down the hall. Could it be her place now? To stand beside Kari, rest a hand on her shoulder. To sit at the foot of a mama's bed and smile, because everything was as it should be. To tell herself what she felt was only happiness, and had nothing in it of grief, of the past rising up to swamp her.

The crowd milled around her. She stood at its center, at once surrounded but alone.

"Thanks be," she whispered. Then she turned from the house and slipped away.

# CHAPTER 6

"Is she sleeping?"

Jena threaded her way between the rows of beds in the Wrapping Center.

After leaving the house, she had walked back through the forest to meet the rest of the line. They would be eager for news of the birth, and she was happy enough to deliver it. But more than that, she wanted to secure the harvest. She was relieved when she had gathered the pouches and slung them across her chest, even more so when she delivered them to the Stores.

Any other day, she would have lingered in the front room where their tunneling gear was kept—adding to the maps and checking the rope for signs of wear, the pouches for fraying. They could ill afford to have the rope fail as they descended a shaft or to lose the hard-won harvest through a hole. But when she had given the last of the pouches to Berta, the Mother fixed her with a look. "The rest can wait, child. Go and be with your sister."

*Your sister.* There was no hesitation in Berta's words. It was so easy, Jena thought, for others to smooth over her past, to add her cleanly to another family as if her own had never existed.

"Kari?" Jena's voice was muted. The Center was a place that demanded hushed tones, careful footfalls. Even if the baby wasn't asleep, another girl might be. Even those who had long outgrown naps fell asleep here; the hours of stillness induced a lethargy that was hard to resist.

Kari raised a finger to her lips, gesturing into the crib with her other hand.

The baby was wrapped properly now, the soft fabric overlapping in a regular crisscross pattern around her body. *Like a cocoon,* Jena thought. Beneath the outer wrappings there would be another layer, this one encasing each limb separately, pressing firmly around the flesh.

It was a long time since she and Kari had been wrapped like this. The schedule changed as a girl grew—both in the number of hours and the way she was wrapped. By the time she was six, she need hardly come here at all; as long as she wore the inner wrappings under her normal clothes, that was enough. At the monthly measurings, the Mothers would check that the material was wound properly, but otherwise they trusted the mamas to manage their own daughters. A girl who joined the line earned her family a generous allocation of mica that would see them safely through the winter. There were allocations of food and medicine too, but it was the mica that mattered most. While everything else could be bartered—a day's labor for some extra potatoes, a few blankets for some smoked rabbit—trade in mica was strictly forbidden. Each household had to manage on its allocation, and they all knew how fine a point survival could turn on when the thaw came late. No one would jeopardize their daughter's prospects by taking liberties with the schedule.

"Isn't she perfect?" Kari said. "Papa said she looks like me. I don't know, though."

Jena ran a hand along the rough wood of the crib. Papa Dietz was right. There was something of Kari in the baby, something about her eyes—the neat pekoe-nut shape of them, the slight crinkling at the edges as if they were on the verge of a smile.

She felt a rush of tenderness. This little one. She and Kari would keep her safe. They would hold her close and protect her. And teach her, later—about the maze and the mountain and the work of the harvest. The years tumbled through Jena's mind. Seven would pass before the child could join the line. Jena tried to picture herself then, at twenty-one. It was not so very old; if she were careful, she might still be tunneling then.

"You should have come in," Kari said. "Mama was asking for you."

"How is she?"

"She's good. The Mothers said she'll be fine." Kari's expression lightened. "And Papa . . . you should have seen him. He's so proud. I thought he was going to bust out of his skin."

Jena couldn't help but smile. Papa Dietz had always worn his feelings right on the surface.

She extended a hand, thinking to stroke the baby's downy fuzz of hair, but then stopped. There was a movement, barely there at first. But then more—eyelids fluttering, eyelashes trembling like the rapid beating of a dragonfly's wings. A wriggling along the torso, the cocoon stretching as the baby made the slow climb out of sleep. And finally a sound, the faintest of mewlings.

"She's waking up!" Kari shot a glance at the back room. Mother Irina was visible through the open door. It looked like she was measuring, as one of the numbered ribbons was draped around her neck and there was a young girl with her.

The baby gave another cry, louder this time, and Irina called out, "I'll just be a minute."

"She said I could feed her." Kari's face was bright. "We can take turns if you want."

"It's all right. You do it."

The baby had begun to squirm inside her wrappings. Not against them—it was too soon for that—but simply in the way you reach out when you first wake, finding your own borders again.

Irina came through from the back room with a bottle and spoon in one hand. The girl she had been measuring followed, her wrappings now covered by a rough cotton dress. She lingered a moment, perhaps hoping for a glimpse of the baby, but Irina made a shooing motion with her free hand. "Off you go."

As the girl scampered away, Irina passed the bottle to Kari. It was less than a third full, perhaps a dozen small spoonfuls. "Just a little at a time. Don't let her hurry you. She'll cry for more, but you have to be firm. You have to—"

"I know." There was an impatient edge to Kari's voice. No tunneler needed Irina to tell her about feeding schedules. About wanting more—always more—until eventually you learned to hold the hunger at arm's reach so that it hovered outside you. Still there, but bearable. Worth it.

As if on cue, the baby drew in a swift breath and wailed, an outraged sound that rang up to the ceiling timbers and spread out to fill the room.

"She can smell it." Irina motioned to a chair by the window. "Sit down. I'll bring her in a minute."

When Kari hesitated, Irina clicked her tongue. "Go on. It won't hurt her to wait." She fussed with the baby for a few minutes, checking her wrappings and stretching the measuring tape against her, then carried her to the chair.

Kari cradled the baby and scooped spoonfuls of milk into her mouth. The delicate lips pursed in and out in a sucking motion. Sometimes they knocked against the spoon, spilling droplets of milk across her cheeks and chin.

When she had settled into a rhythm, Kari relaxed and sighed. "She's so small."

Jena put a hand on Kari's shoulder, gave her the slightest of squeezes.

"I wonder if she'll be a cleanskin."

"If the rock allows it."

"Of course," Kari said quickly. "I just . . . I hope so. It would be easier."

They fell silent for a while, the only sound the occasional snort or splutter as Kari spooned drops of milk into the baby's mouth. Jena placed a hand on the tiny head. It was so perfect like this, so right. There was something in her that wanted to close the circle—one hand on Kari, the other on the baby, making a space into which no one else could enter, if only for this moment.

There was an odd movement then, the baby's scalp seeming to pulse beneath Jena's hand. As her fingers probed gently, she remembered. There were thin plates here that took time to knit together. Until the bone sealed itself, there was this fragile border between inside and out. And so you could feel it—*the heart beating in the head*. Was it her own papa who had told her this, or Papa Dietz? She had been so young when Kari's family took her in that she sometimes had trouble separating memories of one from the other. But she did know this: that it would take only the slightest pressure to rupture it. It made her queasy to think on it.

She looked past Kari, through the window on the

far side of the room. Light slanted through the open shutters and played across the nearby beds. Outside, people hurried past, heading for the center of the village. A thin line of smoke rose above the Square, and it was toward this that they flocked, but there was no threat this time, no cause for alarm.

Kari inclined her head in the direction of Jena's gaze. "Do you think they'll roast a bird?"

"Maybe two." It had been a day. It was the least the village could do to welcome such a daughter.

The baby began to fret. The bottle was empty. Kari dropped the spoon inside, where it came to rest with a hollow clatter. Then she smiled down at her sister, her arms tightening around her.

"All gone," she cooed softly. "No more."

✳

"Another bowl?"

Father knows what Lia's answer will be. He ladles more stew from the pot without waiting for a reply.

Lia breathes in the steam that rises from the glistening surface. The stew is mouthwatering—rich and full of flavor. Ripe tomatoes have colored it a deep red, and Father has added juicy chunks of orange and yellow peppers. Lia has seen where these grow; there is a farm on the other side of Shorehaven that she passes on her way to the mountain. Brightly colored vegetables stand in seemingly endless rows, their skins ablaze in the sun, which rises from the ocean and drenches the plains until late into the afternoon.

"I'll take some too." Mother holds out her bowl. "That was a good, plump bird."

"I set the snare again," Lia says. "Maybe I'll get another tomorrow."

"So soon?" Father raises his eyebrows.

"Maybe." Lia blows onto her stew, then lifts a thick spoonful to her mouth. Though there is no shortage of landbirds on the island, they usually take longer to trap. But lately she has been setting her snare by the mountain, where people seldom go. Perhaps it is that the birds there are less wily, more trusting. Perhaps it is simply that there are more of them.

Father says that one day he will teach Lia how to loose an arrow, to fell a skybird, but she is not sure she wants to learn. There is something about seeing them soar that makes her heart lift; it feels wrong to bring them down.

She takes a mouthful of stew, chews slowly. The bird is tender on her tongue, the juices thick and satisfying. She sets her spoon down, slipping it into the broth like a fisherman drops a line into the ocean.

"Tomorrow," she says.

# CHAPTER 7

"Three!" Calla clapped her hands. "Can you believe it?"

She was standing by Jena at the long table where food for the feast had been laid out. Large platters were piled high with spiced yams and vegetables and fresh bread from the bakery. There was baked fish and a heavy pot of rabbit stew. And directly in front of them sat three plump birds, fresh off the spit. As they watched, one of the Mothers took up a knife and began to carve.

Calla jiggled on the balls of her feet, her gaze fixed eagerly on the meat.

"Just a little," Jena cautioned. "We'll go inside again soon."

"I know that." Calla turned to Jena. "Still . . . it's good, isn't it?"

Though most would not get to taste them, just seeing the birds made something in you sing. Since their ancestors, accustomed to abundance, had hunted out the landbirds generations ago, skybird had become their most precious meat. A skybird was not like a fish or a rabbit. You could not just set a snare or cast a net and wait for the hapless creature to stumble in. A skybird called for a keen eye, an unerring arrow. To have one at a feast was luxury enough; for there to be three spoke of the value the Mothers placed on this tiny new life.

Jena watched as the soft slices of flesh fell away from the bone. When she was little, she had felt sorry for the birds — one minute wheeling high above, the next plunging groundward. When one fell from the sky, the others would scatter for a moment, circling, and then resume formation, taking up the empty space as if it had never been there.

There was something sad about that thought, but natural too. A thing gone was a thing gone. There was nothing those that remained could do but observe the loss, fly on.

"Forty and forty," Calla breathed. "I can't even imagine."

"Oh, you should see her. She —"

"Jena? Do you want mash?" The familiar voice made Jena start. Petria stood on the other side of the table, a serving spoon in one hand, a plate in the other. Until last week, she had been one of them, tucked into the center of the line. Now it was as if she had always been elsewhere. Her hair hung loose around her face; she scooped yam mash from the pot with an easy confidence.

Before Jena could reply, the Mother who had been carving began piling slices of meat onto the plate. "Of course she'll take some, child. And plenty of it."

Calla raised an eyebrow. "I thought we were going inside soon."

Jena flushed. "It's not for me. It's—"

"I know," Calla said. "I'm teasing."

The others were back at the house. Though everyone loved a feast, Mama Dietz was too tired to come out. Kari was keeping her company while Papa Dietz made soup. With the food Jena brought back, they would have their own feast, just the four of them.

Once Calla had her plate, Jena turned from the table and began making her way through the crowd of people that thronged nearby.

"Will you sit for a while?" Calla gestured at the fire pit in the center of the Square. Low benches ringed

67

its perimeter; later, people would gather there with their meals, talking and celebrating deep into the night. The rough flagstones nearby were burnished by the firelight, glowing with a warmth that made them seem almost alive. Orange fingers of flame reached skyward; some spiraled into smoke while others curled back upon themselves, collapsing into embers.

The sight sent Jena's hand instinctively to her chest, but then she relaxed. The mica was well away, safe in the Stores. It was another irony of life in the valley that the substance they relied on for warmth could not be exposed to fire; it must be struck but never lit. Set alight, mica would burn itself out rapidly, uselessly. A single stray spark could see the harvest wasted.

"Jena?"

She shook her head. "They'll be waiting at home."

Calla glanced at Jena's plate and then back to the table. "It's so strange seeing Petria. I can't believe she's thickening. She looks the same to me."

"You can't always tell. The Mothers wouldn't pull her without reason."

"Of course." Calla paused. "She said she might learn to mill grain. Can you imagine?"

Jena couldn't imagine anything but the tunnels, though she supposed she must eventually. No matter how careful you were, you could not keep nature at bay forever. The thickening would come to all of them one day, and while for some it was hardly noticeable, even a small change was enough to put the line at risk. When the Mothers found your numbers moving upward in that telltale way, they would pull you from the line and relax the regimen—no more wrapping, no more need to count every mouthful. It would not be long then before you began to bleed, and to think of your own daughters—more use to the village as a mama than a tunneler once the thickening set in.

"I wonder how they'll manage over winter." Calla plucked a string bean from her plate and began to chew one end slowly.

"They'll be all right," Jena reassured her. Though Petria had left the line, she had tunneled three seasons. When making the Wintering allocation, the Mothers would consider that, along with the hope of future daughters.

On the other side of the Square, Petria ladled scoop after scoop from the pot.

"Maybe she'll become a Mother," Calla said with a half smile.

Jena did not reply. It was the mountain that would decide, and yet they both knew Petria would never be a Mother. It was the heaviest of responsibilities they bore—for allocations, for the harvest, for everything on which the survival of the village rested. A Mother must be close to the mountain so it might speak through her; no girl who had tunneled fewer than six seasons had ever been chosen.

"How about the new one? Will you keep her?"

"Yes." The firmness of her own reply caught Jena by surprise. "She'll do well."

"Have you told her? I can do it if you want." Calla turned to scan the crowd.

"It's all right. I'll talk to her tomorrow."

It was a pleasant thought. The news that a girl had been accepted into the line was always welcome, but would be more so this time. *A sixth child. A first daughter.* It would mean a lot to have a tunneler in such a family.

They said good night, and Jena made her way to the edge of the Square. Occasionally, someone caught her eye and murmured, "Congratulations!" or "It is a day." But most people were gathered by the table, waiting for their chance at a plate. It was understood that tunnelers were served first; after that, a rambling line had formed. No one wanted to be on the end of it, mouth watering for meat while only yams remained.

Jena was almost clear of the Square when she felt

a hand on her arm. A low voice muttered something indistinct.

"Thanks be," she replied. For the most part, this was as good an answer as any. But in response, there was a soft laugh. She turned to see a familiar face framed against the orange glow from the Square. The effect was an odd one, as if the boy were lit from the inside.

"I asked if you were all right," Luka said. "Funny way to reply."

"I didn't hear you. I just thought . . ."

"So are you, then?"

"All right? Why wouldn't I be?"

Luka shrugged. "Berta said you were tired. She was going to make you a tonic."

"I don't need a tonic. I'm fine."

It was true. What had happened that afternoon already felt far away, like a dream that had receded.

"That's what I said." Luka grinned. "I told her how tough you are. She said she knew but you could still use a tonic."

Jena returned his smile. Although the long hours of wrapping and training meant that girls tended to keep to themselves, as Berta's grandson, Luka was often around, and over the years they had developed an easy rapport.

"Anyway, congratulations. Forty and forty."

His words did not call for a reply. There was something to simply hearing the numbers. Jena looked down, taking in the compact sweep of her own body. She herself had been forty-four, forty-six, numbers that had made the village gasp back then. But babies had been coming earlier lately, and smaller. Perhaps there would be a day when a girl began with thirty, when forty didn't earn you a bird and fifty was enough to make people spit on the ground.

"Six moons." Luka gave a low whistle. "You should have seen the Mothers getting everything ready last night. They were so excited."

"Last night?" Jena's eyes widened. She hadn't realized Mama Dietz had labored through the night. It must have started after she and Kari had gone to bed; they always turned in early when they were tunneling and rose before dawn, slipping out soundlessly almost before they were fully awake. Even if Papa Dietz had heard them, he would have said nothing, not wanting to worry them, knowing they must keep their thoughts on the harvest.

Jena considered the thick slices of bird on her plate with satisfaction. There was strength in there, and that was what a mama needed after a birthing.

"I should go." She gestured down the darkened street.

"Me too. Berta said she'd save me a mouthful of bird." Luka looked back toward the Square. The table was all but invisible in the midst of the swarming crowd. "See you around, then. You're not going inside tomorrow, are you?"

"No," Jena began, "but . . ." *I'll be busy,* she was going to say. *With Min and the baby and Mama Dietz.* But Luka was already moving away, and so she did the same, turning her back on the fire and the feast and hurrying away down the narrow road toward the rock wall, toward home.

# CHAPTER 8

"There you are!"

Papa Dietz's voice was chiding, but gentle all the same. He was stirring a shallow pot on the hearth, steam rising as he turned the spoon in slow, lazy circles. The liquid inside was a pale brown, so thin as to be almost clear.

"How's the soup?" Jena asked.

Kari flashed her a wry smile. "How do you think?"

"This should help." Jena slid her plate onto the table.

"So much bird! That's very generous." Papa Dietz lifted the spoon, letting a stream of liquid fall onto the soup's surface. Aside from his porridge, it was the least appetizing thing Jena had ever seen.

"Where's Mama Dietz?"

He nodded down the hall. "She'll be along soon. You should go and see her, though. We missed you earlier."

"I know. I—"

"It's all right. Go on."

The door was ajar but not wide open. Jena knocked gently and waited.

"Who's that knocking in her own home? Come on in!"

Though Mama Dietz's tone was light, it was shot through with weariness. She was sitting on the edge of the bed. Her nightshirt was unbuttoned, and she had one hand at her breast, squeezing. The other hand held a bottle, and with every stroke of her fingers, fat droplets of milk fell into its open neck. As Jena came in, her face softened. "I'm glad to see you."

Jena approached the bed. "How are you?"

"Tired. But well, I think."

"Was it hard?"

"It's always hard. It is the way of these things." She gave one final stroke and then set the bottle down on the bedside table. It was about half full, a creamy yellow tide line circling the container's transparent perimeter. As the liquid seemed to bead and thicken, Jena felt her stomach lurch.

What Kari had given the baby today was a paler version of this, thinned with boiled water. When a daughter was new, it was important she have milk from the breast. It was full of things to make her strong, to turn her eyes to the world and make her thirst for the life it offered. But it was also rich. Too much, too soon, was not good for a daughter. Acquired early, a taste for fat was difficult to unlearn.

Mama Dietz clipped a lid onto the bottle. She shrugged her shirt back across her chest and began fastening the buttons. Jena couldn't help casting a sideways glance. Even through the coarse material, the outline of her heavy breasts was unmistakable.

Had it been the same for her own mama? She supposed it had. But how strange it must be to have your body swell beyond you like that. First the belly and then the breasts, and things never quite returning the way they had been, even when the baby was long grown.

There was no need to think on such things, though. Jena showed no signs of thickening early, and people said her mama had been the same. She had tunneled sixteen seasons before Jena was born, the longest of anyone before or since.

Like mama, like daughter, Jena hoped. Mother

Irina had said as much once when she was measuring her at the Center. She had clicked her tongue as she stretched out the tape. *It comes easy to you, doesn't it?*

At six, Jena had heard only praise in the Mother's voice. By the time she realized that there might have been something else, the day was long past.

"Perhaps you could take this to Irina in the morning?" Mama Dietz slid the bottle toward Jena. "She'll need more and I wouldn't mind sleeping in. Actually" — she reached to the floor beside the bed — "you could take this to Berta too."

It was a different sort of bottle — long and brown, with a cork stopper in the end. There was no milk in this one, just the final dregs of a thick, dark liquid congealed at its base.

"What is it?"

"I'm not sure," Mama Dietz replied. "Just something she gave me yesterday. After a while you stop asking. It seems like every time you turn around, there's a Mother holding a bottle. Something for nausea, or strength, or to help you sleep. I wonder if they do much of anything, really." She gave a faint smile. "Still, I can't say I wasn't glad of a good night's sleep this morning. I couldn't believe it when the pains started." She rose slowly to her feet.

As Jena reached for the bottle, something struck her. "This morning?"

"I thought they were just cramps at first. It was so early, I thought they couldn't possibly be the real thing." Mama Dietz gave a rueful laugh.

"So you didn't labor overnight?"

"No, thanks be. This one was short and sharp." Mama Dietz hesitated. "Is something wrong?"

Jena realized she was frowning. "No. It's just . . ." She was thinking of what Luka had said about the Mothers. About how excited they had been last night, thinking a six-moon baby was coming. But if the pains hadn't begun until this morning, then . . .

She shook her head. "It's nothing."

Maybe Luka had simply misspoken. Or perhaps it was just another of those strange things about the Mothers. Sometimes there was no explanation for the things they seemed to know.

Mama Dietz threaded her last button into place. "All right. Shall we eat, then?"

Jena took Mama Dietz's arm for the walk down the hall. In the kitchen, she put the bottles into the cool-box by the door and then followed Mama Dietz to the table. Once they were seated, Papa Dietz set a bowl of soup and a plate of bird and vegetables in front of each of them.

"Goodness!" Mama Dietz exclaimed. "How many did they roast?"

"Three."

"Three! Well, it is a day, after all. Forty and forty."

"She's so small," Kari said. "Papa says she's like me, but my numbers were nothing like that. Her nose is different too. And her hair's so dark."

"Hair often changes color," Mama Dietz said. "Yours was red at first."

"*Red?*"

Papa Dietz nodded. "Like wickerberry it was. And lots of babies start out fair, then get darker."

Kari reached for the end of Jena's braid and ran her fingers through the dark strands. "How about Jena? Was she . . . *oh.*" She flushed. "Sorry."

Mama Dietz put her hand on Jena's. "You were never fair. I remember when you were born. You had this serious little face, all wrinkled and puckered, like a tiny old Mother. And dark eyes and dark hair, from the very first day."

Of course Mama Dietz would know. She and Jena's mama had been friends since they were children, and even though Mama Dietz hadn't lasted long as a tunneler, they had remained so. It was why Jena and Kari had been so close. It was why the Dietzes had

79

taken Jena in when she had nowhere else to go.

Mama Dietz looked steadily into Jena's eyes. "Your mama loved you so much, Jena. She would be very proud of you."

"Your papa too," Papa Dietz added quietly.

Something fragile seemed to hover between them. No one talked about Papa anymore, and somewhere inside her, Jena had come to find that a relief. There was no way of explaining what he had done and no point trying. It was easier to simply forget, to move on and hope others would do the same.

Mama Dietz squeezed Jena's hand, then released. "I heard it was a good harvest."

"Better than good," Papa Dietz said. "Perhaps we'll be all right this year."

*We.* It was the slipperiest of words. Was it the family he meant, or the village? For most of the year they were nearly the same thing, everyone pulling together, making things work. But when the snow came, the world narrowed to four walls and a roof, to a "we" that spoke only of those within arm's reach.

"Thanks be." Mama Dietz finished the last of the soup and set her bowl to one side.

Kari slid hers across the table. "Here, have this." The bowl was still close to half full, and she had scarcely touched the plate Jena brought.

"I've had enough." Kari sat back, one hand patting her stomach.

It was an old gesture, a carryover from the past that had become something of a joke. People used to do this after meals, they said. Only instead of saying *enough,* they would say *full.* They would rub their stomachs, declaring *I'm full,* as if it were something to be pleased about. As if taking more than you needed were something to be proud of. *Oh, I could just burst.* Sometimes they would loosen their belts so they could stuff more in.

"Enough?" Mama Dietz said gently. Even this was a word not often heard in the valley.

"I'm fine, Mama."

"All right, then." Mama Dietz took up her spoon gratefully.

Kari exchanged a look with Papa Dietz. He leaned forward, sliding his arms toward Jena across the table. "We thought to name her."

*Already?* Jena didn't need to say it. To name a daughter barely a day old was an act of great faith or great folly. Perhaps both. Giving someone a name might pull them toward you, into the world. But if it did not, it would make their loss more difficult to bear.

Kari's eyes met hers. "She's strong, Jena."

"Ailin," Mama Dietz said. "That's what we were thinking."

Jena caught her breath. "It's beautiful." It was, but it was risky too, if risky was the right word. *Little stone.* It was a name that made a girl part of the mountain. She would have to be a tunneler or live at odds with herself for the length of her days. It would be a cruel thing, with such a name, to spend your life baking or plowing fields. But still, not so different perhaps from the many girls given names meaning "slender" and "slim" who grew far beyond their family's hopes, and ended up doing the same.

She looked around the table. *We,* Papa Dietz had said. That word again.

"It's perfect," she said finally.

Mama Dietz reached for her hand once more. "I'm so glad you like it."

Papa Dietz and Kari put their hands in too, placing them on top.

"Ailin." Papa Dietz gave the name a finality, as if something that had been shifting had now settled, taking on its final shape.

"Ailin," Mama Dietz repeated softly.

Jena imagined her saying it thousands of times in the years to come. *Ailin, breakfast is ready. Time for bed,*

*Ailin. Ailin, this needs to be tighter. Just one more mouthful, Ailin.*

*Keep your head down, Ailin. Follow. The others will show you the way. It is a day. Thanks be. The rock has allowed it.*

"Ailin," said Jena, and the word sounded right and good on her tongue. "It's perfect," she said again, and prayed it would be so.

✳

*Jena is four, perhaps five.*

*No, she is five.*

*Her birthday has slipped past unremarked upon. Unnoticed.*

*There has been no present — no doll stuffed with dried beans or straw. No rough-cut chunk of rabbit roasting on a spit in the hearth.*

It is all right, *she tells herself. She doesn't need a doll, because she has something better — a tiny sister, all her own.*

Priya. Alana. Sian.

*She has so many ideas, but when she tells Papa, he shakes his head.*

It is too early, *he says.* The baby is weak. The weight of a name will be too heavy upon her.

*Still, they tumble through Jena's head, weave quietly through her dreams.*

Ilona. Caren.

*Some are pretty and others strong. It has something to do with the way they end — some are open, reaching into sky, while others are sure and steady, like stone.*

Give my sister a strong name, *she thinks.* Give her a name that will keep her here with us.

*It is two moons since Mama went in the ground. There is a chill in the air and a ring of white on the tips of the mountain's fingers.*

*Sometimes Papa takes Jena to the place where she lies. Jena strokes the pebble they have chosen from the spring. Rollers are allowed too, and crumblers — stones the mountain has released from itself. But water stones are the best. They are cool and smooth. They come from a quiet place, and that seems right for Mama, for this.*

*Papa sits there too long, the Mothers say. She has heard them talking while she lies in the Center. It will be Wintering soon; he should be climbing across roofs with his hammer and nails, plugging holes, crisscrossing planks of wood one upon the other.*

I'm five, *she says to Papa one morning. It is important that he knows. She may not get a doll or a rabbit, but nothing can stop the numbers. She is glad to be five. It is one year closer to seven, and seven is what everybody wants. Seven is when you start training in the maze, then the shallow tunnels. Seven is one year away from taking your place in the line, if they choose you.*

*They will choose her. Jena knows it as surely as spring follows even the longest of winters. As surely as the numbers that move upward year upon year.*

*She has been good about her wrapping. She has lain still at the Center without squirming or complaining. And when she is out, she has been keeping her muscles strong, doing all the exercises the Mothers say she must.*

*But when she tells Papa, his face is blank. He looks through her, his eyes somewhere else.*

*Later, he comes to the Center. She hears his voice and turns her head, but there are beds in the way, and cribs after that. She can't see anything, but she knows it is him. She strains her ears toward the sound, but a baby is crying and it is hard to hear. There is something strange in his voice, something Jena has never heard before. It sounds like he is trying to whisper, but he is shouting.*

*A door flings wide and there are footsteps heavy in the room, stamping up and down the aisles between the beds.*

*Arms reach out, but they are not for Jena. A baby cries and then another. He is picking something up, a small bundle.*

*No. He mustn't. A new daughter needs to lie still, to learn to be only with herself.*

*Then the Mothers are there. Different arms reaching now. Reaching and taking. Soothing and settling.*

*She can't hear his voice anymore. But there are glimpses. An* arm on his — wiry and thin against his own thick flesh. They are leading him away. But he is all right now — not shouting, not arguing. He is soothed and settled and Jena is glad. Because she knows this feeling. Sometimes something flares inside her — the wrappings feel impossibly tight; an arm wants to throw itself this way, a leg to kick out.

But the Mothers are always there. They sit by your bedside, stroke your wayward limbs until the restlessness subsides. I know, they croon. I know. And you know they do, because they walked this path before you. So you become settled again. Calm.

Papa is all right now. The Mothers will take care of him.

When they unwrap her later, Jena goes to the baby's crib. She is sleeping again, so quiet, so still.

Seren.

The name comes to her like a secret.

But when she tells Papa at dinner, he shakes his head. Later, he says. After.

After what?

Papa does not reply. He turns slowly and looks out toward the mountain. He ladles soup from the pot and says, Eat, Jena. You will need your strength.

# CHAPTER 9

"Min?"

Jena had risen early, unable to sleep. She found herself eager to deliver the good news, to see the look on the younger girl's face when she heard she was joining the line.

But as early as Jena had been, Min was earlier. Jena smiled when Min's mama said she would find her here.

She peered into the slit in the mountain's side. It was ages since she had visited this place they called the Source. The passage ahead was dark, but she had tunneled it hundreds of times before and knew every twist and turn. Though it had once extended deep into the mountain, a rockfall had blocked the path and it now formed a closed loop. Whether you went left or right, you would end up back at this point. It was safe but challenging to navigate and was often used in training.

There was a faint scrabbling sound to the left. Jena peered down the tunnel. A finger appeared around the bend, a hand following. A shoulder edged sideways, rotating itself through and out. A slight frame, a tousled head.

"Min?" Jena called. "It's Jena. I . . ."

The head ducked back around the bend in the rock. And now there was a noise to Jena's right. She turned and saw Min emerging from the other end of the tunnel.

"Oh," Jena said. "I thought . . ." She gestured to her left. "Who else is here?" There must be another girl training, perhaps one who wasn't quite old enough for the Source. "It's all right," she called. "You're not in trouble."

But the head stayed lowered and the figure did not move. Jena turned back to Min. "Who is it?" she repeated. "Tell her she can come out. I won't . . ."

Min's face was white. She scrambled to where Jena sat, her eyes wide. "I didn't know," she said. "He must have followed me." She leaned past Jena, her strained voice echoing across the stone. "Come out of there!"

Jena felt suddenly as if all the warmth had drained from her body. *He?*

The shape came slowly toward them, fearful eyes flicking up and down. It was one of Min's brothers, a friend of Luka's. Jena had seen them skylarking about in the Square. He was an odd-looking boy—slim and pale in a way that made him seem almost ghostly.

But it didn't matter which boy it was. Only that it was a boy—inside the mountain, where no boy, no man, must ever go.

"You can't be here, Thom!" Min's voice was shaking. "I'm so sorry, Jena. I—"

"It's not her fault!" the boy said quickly. "She didn't know."

Panic flooded Jena. "Get out!" It took everything in her not to crawl down and haul him roughly from the tunnel.

When he was out, perched in front of her on the ledge below the opening, she turned on him. "You can't go in there! What were you thinking?" A knot snarled in her chest, fear and anger coursing through her in equal measure.

"I didn't go far," he protested. "I just went in for a second. I was coming straight out again."

Jena fought to keep her voice level. "It doesn't matter. You know that."

"I'm sorry. I just . . ." Thom hesitated. "Min was talking about it last night. I wanted to see what it felt like."

"I wasn't bragging," Min said. "It was because of Mama. She never got to tunnel. I just . . . I wanted her to know."

"Please," Thom urged. "Don't tell anyone. I won't do it again."

A moment hung in the air between them, deciding which way it would turn. After a long minute, Jena took a deep breath. "Go. And don't come back here."

Thom was over the ledge almost before she finished speaking. He scrambled down, a shower of grit and small stones accompanying his rapid descent. She winced as he half climbed, half fell to the ground below, but he did not seem hurt. A boy did not break the way a girl might. There was something surer about their bodies, less brittle about their bones.

Jena waited until his retreating shape had disappeared into the trees before turning to Min. *Don't tell anyone,* Thom had said. And they both knew who he meant.

She considered. The fault was Thom's alone, but

Jena knew only too well how the transgressions of one might fall upon another.

"The Mothers don't have to know," she said finally. "But it can't happen again."

"It won't," Min said quickly. "Thank you."

"Don't thank me. If judgment comes, it will be from the mountain." She leaned back against the rock, her heart pounding: a boy inside the rock, and here of all places. It went against everything they had been taught, everything they knew.

It was men who had dug into the mountain, angering the earth. Men who had brought about Rockfall and the wall of water that had followed to destroy their village, their world. Only a handful had survived—those who had been in the shelter of the valley, away from the water and clear of the mountain.

All those men saw was that the mountain had come down. Where their friends had been working was a chaos of twisted stone—no sign of life, no hope of it. But there was more to come, for when they tried to leave the valley, they found themselves trapped.

In the days that followed, they hauled themselves through fissures in the tumbled rock, only to find the way sealed at every turn. They climbed the mountain, casting ropes across its dark face like ragged stitches.

But the slopes were treacherous, the fingers of stone curving into impossible overhangs that thwarted every attempt. And all the while, the mountain trembled and shook, as though it were trying to throw them off. The earth growled beneath them with the guttural sounds of a beast defending its territory, or its life.

About a week had passed when two men standing at the base of this very spot, ropes slack at their sides in despair, heard a different kind of sound. It was a sort of scrabbling, like a scuttler might make, only purposeful somehow, as if there was a will behind it. As if something was in there, trying to get out.

At first, their hearts leaped. Perhaps those who had been working in the mountain that day were not lost after all.

There was someone alive — that much was true. But it was not men whose eyes locked on theirs from an impossible seam in the rock. Not men who pulled themselves clear — dirt-smeared, bleeding.

"I always think about them when I'm here," Min said softly. "The Seven, I mean."

It was as though she were reading Jena's thoughts.

It was from here that the first tunnelers had emerged — though they were not tunneling back then but simply surviving.

Seven women had crawled clear, nose to toe. One man's wife. Another's sister, neighbor.

There was reunion, tears. And then there was grief.

For everything was gone, the women said. Everything and everyone. The earth had opened up and swallowed the village, splintering and tumbling their homes into its gaping maw. And then a wall of water had risen like a fist from the flat surface of the ocean and poured across the land, drowning everything that remained.

These women had been spared only because they were on the higher ground of the Pass. They were about to make their way through into the valley when the water came, surging up and over the lip of the mountain. The sea roared in their ears as the stone walls began to crack and sway around them, as wall became roof and crashed upon them, sealing them inside.

They hauled themselves through the jagged dark as the mountain rumbled, sending tremors through the rock that blocked each passage behind them. Until finally they were here, seven women emerging from the stone as if it had opened up to let them through.

The mountain could hardly have sent them a clearer message. Men had dug into the mountain and women had crawled clear. Those first Seven had become the Mothers of them all.

Min turned to Jena. "It's all right, isn't it . . . that I told Mama about being inside? She always wanted to tunnel." She hesitated. "She tried for eight years."

Jena stared at Min in disbelief. It wasn't odd that her mama had kept trying. Jena had seen girls like this. Determined girls. Desperate girls. Girls who wrapped themselves tighter and tighter, who said no to a second helping — or a first — then returned to run the maze for a third year, a fourth. But eight?

"I just wanted to tell her about it," Min went on. "I never thought Thom would —"

"It's all right." Jena met Min's eyes. "You did well yesterday."

"Thank you."

Jena was glad to hear no false modesty in the girl's voice. No *Really? Do you think so?* No reaching for more praise.

"I was a bit scared at first." Min hesitated. "No, not scared. It's just . . . it's so different. Outside feels so close here, but where we were yesterday . . . it's like you could almost forget the world, like the rock is all there is."

Jena felt a rush of affection for the girl. What she said was so . . . *right.* Or at least it was exactly how Jena had felt after her first harvest. And felt to this day, more strongly than ever.

"Did you need me for something?" Min asked. "Did I miss something yesterday? Loren showed me how to check the gear. I thought I did everything, but . . ."

"I'm sure it's fine. You can show me tomorrow."

Jena watched as understanding bloomed across Min's face. "Tomorrow?"

"You'd better grow your hair a bit. It makes it easier to braid."

"Oh." Min's shoulders sagged with relief. "Mama will be so happy. It's been hard."

How could it be otherwise? Although a daughter earned you extra food and mica, it could hardly be enough to keep five growing boys. But a daughter in the line? That might come close, if you were careful.

*If the rock allowed it.*

"Will your mama not try for another daughter?"

Something passed across Min's face. "It's too dangerous. She's broken."

*Broken.* There was something brittle about the word, and Jena could not make her lips form a reply. All she could see was a body worn thin by the years, splintering, shattered.

She turned and put a hand on Min's arm. As she brushed the rock, there was a crunching sound, the sudden feeling of something sharp against her side.

She thrust a hand into her pocket. It was the bottle Mama Dietz had given her; she had forgotten to return it when she took the milk. When she withdrew her hand, it held jagged shards of glass. And there was that smell again—faint but distinct. The cloying sweetness that had hung in the hallway yesterday, and on her mama's breath all those years ago.

Something twisted inside her. She was glad of the rock at her back, calm and still.

Min wrinkled her nose. "What is that?"

Jena forced a note of lightness into her voice. "Just a tonic Mama Dietz had."

"For the birthing? I think my mama had that."

A birthing tonic? Jena supposed it must be. Still, there was something odd about what Min had said. One daughter. A mama who had broken.

It came to her suddenly. "How do you know?"

"What do you mean?" Min looked puzzled.

"You said your mama had it for a birthing . . . but I thought you were the youngest?"

"Oh. No, it wasn't me. It was when Mama . . ." Min's voice faltered. "It was a few years ago. She and Papa wanted to try for another daughter, like you said. But something went wrong. The baby stopped moving inside her. At first Mama said it was probably sleeping, but then it kept on until Papa said no baby slept that long—not inside or outside of a mama—and she must go and see the Mothers. They put their hands on her and then that funny thing they listen with. And they said it had died." Tears welled in the corner of her eyes. "They gave Mama something to make the pains start so she could birth it. I saw them bring it out later, wrapped in a blanket."

"A daughter?"

"They wouldn't say. They said it wasn't anything yet, that we shouldn't think on it. But sometimes when I close my eyes I can see its face—so perfect and small." Min lowered her voice to a whisper. "It wasn't nothing. But anyway, it was dead. And all I could think about was how tiny it was, and how good it would have been to have a sister like that. And then Mama was so sick, after. The Mothers said she was badly broken and must never try again."

"I'm so sorry." Their losses were not the same, but Jena knew what it was like—to have that precious bundle in a blanket, to see it slip beyond your reach.

She blinked hard. She would not let her thoughts trip back there again.

"I . . ." she began, then stopped. *Should go and see Berta,* she meant to say. Even without the bottle to return, there was gear to be checked and maps to be charted. But here was that liquid, sticky on her fingers. And Min's words ringing in her ears.

*Something to make the pains start.*

The morning seemed to slow and still. The birdsong from the forest was suddenly distant, the drumming of her heart impossibly loud. This bottle, that smell, the one that ten years ago had colored Mama's final breaths.

*A tonic. Strength for the birthing.* The Mothers' excitement, hours before the pains had started. A six-moon baby. So early, too early. Unless it lived, and then . . .

*Thanks be.*

*The rock has allowed it.*

The thought twisted in her mind. No. It couldn't be.

A birthing tonic because they knew a birthing was coming.

Because they were making it come?

# CHAPTER 10

Under the thick canopy of forest, the clearing was deep in shadow. Although trees had been felled here, those that ringed the space had grown out across it, seeming to reach for each other.

Jena entered softly, her feet nimble across the leaf-strewn ground. She had not meant to come to this place, had scarcely known she was doing so until she found herself skirting its edges.

There had been a point at which she veered from the path, telling Min to go on ahead of her to the Stores. Now that Min was in the line, she must go and see Berta and claim her allocation. Under normal circumstances, Jena would have been eager to accompany her. Most in the village would never be permitted to visit the mica room, and it was a memorable occasion when a new tunneler did so. Unless she went on to lead the line, it would happen only once; for Jena, there was something special about standing beside a girl, watching her take it all in. But right now she could not imagine being in the same room with Berta. She could not look at her and think the things she was thinking.

She cast her eyes to the ground. To the rough stones dotted at regular intervals, marking out each small mound, one from the other. There was no stone for Mama, though — not anymore. Would she even be able to find her after all these years?

People had been so angry back then. Angry enough to steal a stone from a grave. Angry enough to come to the Center, demanding that the Mothers unwrap Jena, send her to the fields where she could do no harm.

*She's her papa's daughter. Such a girl cannot possibly be fit for the line!*

The words rang in Jena's mind, as shrill and clear as they had been all those years ago. It felt like she was unraveling. Things she had thought long forgotten were all of a sudden right *there*, bright fibers of memory unspooling. And she had seen how this worked, how it began with one frayed corner, a single loose thread. It seemed harmless at first, because it was just this one small strand, so you tugged it a little, and before long you were pulling and pulling, unstitching the very fabric of things.

She closed her eyes, gathered herself in. Then took a deep breath and opened them again, intent only on the ground in front of her. It was easier, sometimes, not to let your gaze stray to the left or right.

She need not have doubted, for when her eyes lit upon the grassy mound by which she and Papa had spent so many hours, there was no mistaking it. There was no longer even a depression where the stone had been, nothing to say it was ever there. But she knew, and that was enough.

She knelt upon the ground, feeling the dry undergrowth crackle beneath her.

*Mama.* She rubbed the surface of the glass in her pocket. Something to make the pains start . . . was there really such a thing? Min was young. She had been younger then. It was so easy for a child to misunderstand, to get things twisted around.

Jena considered the haphazard rows of grassy mounds. Would there be a stone for a child born still? Would there even be a grave? If there was, it would be so tiny that . . . *oh.* The realization hit her with a clarity so fine it almost hurt.

A baby had died and Min's first thought had been for how small it was. Jena's had been for whether it was a daughter. Neither of those things mattered, and yet they were all that seemed to. How much *more* would they matter to the Mothers? More than the life of a mama? More than the life of a child?

She pressed her finger onto the sharp edge of the glass. Gently at first, and then more firmly. As it pierced her skin, it was not pain she felt, but something like release.

Her hand closed around a piece of the bottle and she withdrew it from her pocket. The side that had struck the rock had shattered and most of the base had sheared away. But the top remained intact, the cork wedged in place. She laid the chunk of glass on the ground, faint droplets of blood welling from her finger.

*That blooming flower.*

She scooped the other pieces out of her pocket and set them down alongside it. Perhaps she might leave them here for Mama. Not a stone, but something all the same.

There would never be a stone for Papa, but there was nothing she could do about that. Nor could she bear to think of it—the way he had stumbled and fallen, the wall of rock lowering itself upon him. Her hand rubbed absently at the knot between her shoulder blades. Beneath her fingers, the scar was cool and smooth.

A noise behind her made her start—a stick, snapping. Perhaps there was a rabbit in the underbrush.

But as she turned, the sound came again, and with it another, louder and steady. Footfalls.

Her instinct was to hide—even after all these years she could not afford to have people thinking this was where her heart lay—but there was nothing but clearing around her. Along the tree line, a dark head flashed between the leaves.

"Jena?"

She felt herself breathe out. "Luka?"

"Thom told me what happened." He ducked his head under some low-hanging branches. Twigs caught briefly on tufts of his hair, making them stick out at odd angles. "I wanted to talk to you. I saw you heading this way as I came along the path."

"I don't usually come here," Jena said. "I just—"

"I know." Luka's eyes met hers. "It's all right."

Still, the guarded feeling lingered. As grateful as Jena was for Luka's assurance, the truth was he didn't know—how precarious things had once been, the effort it had taken for her to win back people's trust. It wasn't only that she had stopped coming here. She had given herself completely to the Mothers, to her training. Sometimes she wrapped herself at home and built a maze from chairs and tables, running it over and over until it came easily—forward, backward, eyes closed. Again. Then she rebuilt it, making the passages narrower, the bends tighter.

She kept her head down and hugged her arms close to her chest. If someone said, *It is a day,* she said, *Thanks be.* If they offered her a bowl, she shook her head. *No, thank you.* Said she wasn't hungry. And never was.

The girl she had been before was gone. Slowly, carefully, she became a new one. Papa and Mama Dietz's daughter. Kari's sister. This was the girl Luka knew, the girl everyone looked up to.

This was the girl she was, wasn't it?

"I won't tell anyone you were here," Luka said. "I just wanted to talk about Thom."

"What about him?"

"Only that . . . it's been tough for them. For him. And I know he acts a bit strange sometimes. But—"

"A bit strange? He was *inside the mountain.* It's tough for lots of people, Luka. You know that."

"He almost died." Luka's voice was soft, as if he

didn't want to say such words too loudly. Perhaps especially not here.

"I know." Had it been this thaw or last? Papa Dietz had cleared their own doorway and set to helping those still snowbound. Jena was with him at a house a few streets over when she turned and saw the boy, stumbling through the streets like a wraith. It had been a lean season and a long winter and with eight mouths under one roof.

"Don't worry," she said finally. "I'm not going to tell. And things will get easier now."

"Min?" Luka's face brightened. "Do they know?"

"I just told her. She's really good, Luka. She'll last. If they're careful, they should be all right."

"His mama broke, you know. It doesn't seem fair."

"I know, but . . ." Jena trailed off. *It is the way,* she ought to say. But the words seemed suddenly hollow.

"The other night," she said. "At the feast . . . you said the Mothers were getting ready for Mama Dietz's birthing the night before."

Luka nodded.

"Are you sure about that?"

"Of course. Why?"

Jena hesitated. Luka was her friend, but he was also Berta's grandson. She could not look at him without being reminded of the old Mother—the piercing blue of his eyes, the firm set of his jaw. She gave what she hoped was a nonchalant shrug. "No reason. I just didn't realize the birthing took that long."

No matter where her thoughts led her, she was still that five-year-old girl, scrambling for her place in the world. She could not say anything, not without proof. She thought of Min, in the mica room with Berta. Of the small room opposite, filled with bottles and jars.

She glanced down at the shards of glass. On the surface of her skin, a fine point of pain shrilled sharp as a needle.

# CHAPTER 11

Moonlight filtered through the clouds, casting a ghostly pale across the cobblestones. Jena skirted the edges of the Square, a shiver rippling through her. In a few hours the sun would begin to rise. The first lazy fingers of light would filter through the Pass, and the line would gather for the harvest.

In a few short hours, a few short feet from here.

She slowed as she reached the cluster of buildings that formed the Stores. Each building had its own particular function; the one she sought had three rooms, each of them forbidden to most in the village. The girls of the line were permitted to enter the first, but only to return or retrieve their tunneling gear. For that purpose—and for that room—alone, Jena had a key. She drew it now from her pocket and slid it into the lock.

The rope and belts were laid out on a bench just inside; pouches hung on hooks nearby, each one packed and ready to go. She closed the door behind her and hurried on.

A short hall now, a single room on each side of it. To the right, the windowless room where the mica was stored. Min would have stood there this afternoon, her eyes wide, watching Berta work by the pale lamplight. It was a wonder seeing so much mica in one place, the way it rippled and spilled across itself, patterns shifting and reforming, the room seeming to hum with its luminous blue glow.

Jena remembered her own first time as if it were yesterday—how Berta had reached for the thick ledger and flipped through, making tiny notes in one column and another. The hemp bags piled on the table around her—some bulging heavily, others collapsed upon themselves.

But the bags were not Jena's concern now. The room she wanted was on the left. From within, its telltale smells bled into the hall, layering one upon the other: the tart sting of citron, the deep musk of yarrow, the fruity sweetness of wickerberry. This was the dispensary, where roots and herbs of all descriptions were ground and mixed, blended into complex combinations known only to the Mothers. Many a time Jena had glanced down the hall and seen Mother Dyan bent over her mortar and pestle, or holding a bottle to the light, weighing and pouring.

This door was locked too, but Jena had considered that. She was her papa's daughter, after all — and Papa Dietz's too. She knew how old wood warped, that a door once tight in its frame would become less so as the years wore on. And these inner doors were less secure than the front entrance, perhaps on the belief that anyone inside would be worthy of trust.

The thought gave her a moment's pause, but only that. She took the thin wedge of wood from her pocket and placed it between the door and the frame, then worked the handle up and sideways, jiggling as she felt it begin to give. The hook slipped clear of the latch. She leaned into the door with her shoulder, easing the old wood forward, and stepped into the dark room.

She closed the door behind her but did not lock it. There was no need just now.

It was dark, but the faint glow of moonlight would have to do. It would be foolish to burn a flame so close to the mica, and equally so to run the risk of being seen.

The walls around her were lined with tall, wide

shelving that sagged with bottles and jars and packets tied with string. Sheaves of paper were piled in unsteady bundles. Thick bunches of dried herbs and roots hung from the ceiling, some as low as head height; it was like walking through a strange, aromatic forest. There was a table in the center of the room with a low stool alongside it. The surface of the table was mottled with patches of red and orange and dotted with piles of powdered residue. Two bowls sat next to a pair of scales, and spoons of various sizes were laid out nearby, one half full. The effect was vaguely unsettling, as if Dyan had been briefly distracted in the midst of something and might return without warning.

The thought spurred Jena to search more purposefully. But there were so many smells competing in the heavy air. Medicine was dispensed according to need, and this was Dyan's busiest time, as she set herself to the task of preparing for the winter ahead.

Jena picked up a slim bottle containing a clear liquid. *Kalite.* It was labeled — they all were — but that meant nothing without knowing the name of what she had smelled, and she could hardly open every container and test them one by one. She felt a wave of despair.

She riffled through the shelf in front of her,

examining the labels. There were names she recognized, which could be quickly eliminated. *Correas leaf,* which she had for a fever two seasons ago. *Gingeria,* familiar from childhood colds. And *willow-wort* too. Berta had dosed her with that in the days after Papa left; the wound on her shoulder had troubled her longer than it should.

It was none of those, she thought, but then caught herself. Hadn't her fever remedy been sweetened with honey? And the gingeria with wickerberry? Didn't the Mothers add elderflower to willow-wort sometimes, to strengthen it?

There were so many possible combinations. Maybe the exact mixture the mamas had been given wasn't even here. Maybe it was something Dyan mixed up fresh only when it was called for.

Jena could not have said how long she stood staring at the densely packed shelves, picking up one bottle after another, willing them to give up their secrets. The light shifted as the night receded. How much longer before people might start to rise? She glanced at the door. There was another shelf just inside the entrance, this one lined not with bottles but with books.

Her heart began to race almost before the thought

had formed. The Mothers and their lists. The ledgers full of names and columns and numbers. Of who got what and how much and when.

Several dusty books leaned against one another on the shelf, but it was the one on top that drew her eye. None appeared to be labeled, but this one was cleaner, as if it had been used more recently. If nothing else, it was a place to start.

She retrieved the ledger and carried it to the table where there was more light, leafing through the pages even before she had set it down. When she reached *Dietz,* she stopped and ran her finger down the columns. It was all here. There were individual entries for each of them. Papa and Mama Dietz's began when they got married, and Jena supposed they had earlier entries from their own families elsewhere. Kari's entry began at birth, and there was a new one just below it. The Mothers had not added a name yet, though — only the numbers. Perhaps they too were waiting, cautious.

Her gaze fell upon her own entry. It was not alongside Kari's as she had expected, but several rows down. A large space had been left between their names, and it was there that Ailin had been added. Keeping the real family together, Jena supposed — her own addition to the household acknowledged but kept separate all the same.

But it was not her record she sought. She peered at the writing next to Mama Dietz's name.

Beside each entry, one column noted the ailment or condition and the next the remedy that had been dispensed, along with a series of numbers. Strength, perhaps, and dosage? There was a third space filled with tightly packed scrawl—almost illegible in places—that appeared to be notes on the progression of the illness or whether the medicine had proved effective. In this way, a picture of each person in the village had been put together. Jena's finger trembled as it traced its way along the lines.

*Greta Dietz.* A fever here. Something for stomach cramps there. A three-day headache eased by feverfew. A pregnancy—Kari. Willow-wort and comfrey during the birthing; some other scrawled names Jena didn't recognize. Pennyroyal? Calendula? She filed the unfamiliar words away in the back of her mind and read on.

Ailin's birth. A six-moon baby. This was the one that mattered.

Some of the remedies were the same as those for Kari's birth, differing only in the numbers alongside them and the accompanying notes. *Fourteen hours. Small tear. Birthed clean. Healed well. No break. No infection.*

But others were different. And there was a note beside one that made Jena catch her breath. Her finger pressed hard onto the page, smudging the ink.

*Ripen at six. Rubus.*

She had almost missed it. Because it wasn't from the birthing, but earlier, immediately following the notation *With child.*

From there, an arrow had been drawn to a series of notes in the margin. *Yarrow 1/2. Raspberry leaf 6ds. Willowbark 2ds.*

She set her hand on the page to hold the place and continued leafing through the ledger. The entries seemed to be roughly alphabetical. If she was right, the one she sought would be near the back. Her fingers felt wooden; it took her several tries to separate the last few pages, to find the one she needed.

*Werner.*

The name returned to her from a distant place. It was not that she had forgotten, but somewhere over the years she had left it behind, locking it away in a dusty corner far from the light.

*Clara Werner. Ripen at seven.*

And there again, that list of ingredients. *Yarrow 3/4.*
*Raspberry leaf 10ds. Willowbark 4ds.*

The numbers were different, but the names were
the same.

She studied the rows that told the story of Mama's
pregnancy. Something for strength, something for
nausea. The birthing, and afterward. Willow-wort.
This last appearing several times—the strongest
painkiller they had, the dosage increasing with each
new entry. Until there were no more entries—not
then, not ever.

Except for an underlined note in the final column:
*Rubus too strong. Reduce dosage?*

Jena gripped the edge of the table, her legs
suddenly weak. Was this what had taken Mama? Not
the mountain but a too-strong medicine? A medicine
given to her by the Mothers to make her . . . *ripen,* like
a piece of fruit they might hasten to the plucking.

*Rubus.*

She turned to the nearby shelf, again scanning
the rows of packets and bottles. *Rubus.* She found
herself repeating the word over and over, as if to
hold on to it.

Searching was no simple matter. There was an

order to things, she realized. Some remedies were sorted according to usage—fever remedies on one shelf, painkillers another—and within that there was a kind of alphabetical order. But when she finally found what she sought, it was not ordered by either type or spelling. It appeared to have been shelved with just one design in mind—that of concealment.

It was a single bottle on the very bottom shelf, tucked in the far back corner behind a clutch of dried roots. It was empty and had been thoroughly cleaned. There was no trace of sticky residue, no smell of any kind. But there was a label, this one unlike the others in that it was not stuck to the bottle with tree sap but tied loosely around the neck with twine.

When Jena picked it up, she noticed a wadded piece of paper wedged in the corner behind it. Some old label, perhaps—discarded and forgotten. But something made her reach for it, and as she drew it out she saw that it wasn't crumpled but folded, neatly and carefully. As if someone had set it there on purpose and might return to it later.

She unfolded it. It was another list of names and scrawled notations, but the light was dim by the floor and she could only make out part of it. *Werner* again, and *Brandt.* And *Armen*? She stood, angling the paper beneath the light coming from the window. But as she did, shadows flickered around her. There was movement outside.

She ducked, crumpling the paper quickly into her pocket. A figure passed the window. A slight frame, its steps short but purposeful.

Jena shoved the bottle back into place and half stumbled, half crawled across the room. If it was Dyan, she would come straight here. If it was Berta, she would go to the room opposite. Either way, Jena had to get out, at least as far as the front room. The Mothers would not question her being there on a harvest morning, but it would be a different matter if they found her here.

Quiet footsteps padded around the corner of the building. Jena raced for the door, grabbing the ledger as she ran and setting it back on the shelf.

It was not until she had jiggled the lock closed again that she realized the piece of paper was still in her pocket. Down the hall, the shape passed the window in the front room. Whoever it was would soon be at the door, sliding their own key into the lock.

A few short steps and Jena was there, reaching for her satchel almost before her last stride landed. She willed her breathing to slow, her hands to stop shaking.

There was silence outside. No key in the lock, no one trying the handle. The door remained shut.

Then a sound, soft. Someone whispering.

Jena edged toward the door.

*Pouch on the left, rope on the right. Knife, head lamp, water. Make the harvest. Find the light.*

Relief washed over her. She reached for the doorknob and twisted.

"Oh!" The figure jumped back.

It was Min. Her hair was tightly braided, her eyes wide. One hand was over her mouth, the other clutched to her chest.

"You're here. I thought I'd be first." She flushed. "I just . . . I couldn't sleep."

Despite everything, Jena felt a smile ghost her own lips. She might have known. A restless night, a foolishly early arrival. Hadn't she been the same when she was new?

She pushed the paper firmly into the bottom of her pocket. The other girls would be along soon. She must put aside the thoughts that careered through her head and settle into the day's familiar rhythms: a coil of rope looped over the shoulder, a belt cinched around the waist, a single chip of mica snapped into each head lamp.

*Make the harvest. Find the light.*

There was something unsettling about how easily her mind turned back to that well-worn path.

"Come inside." She gestured toward the door. "We'll go over your gear."

# Chapter 12

"I'm done."

Loren looped the drawstring around the neck of her pouch and drew the ends together in a secure knot. The area they were harvesting was illuminated by all seven head lamps, each making its own halo of light. They were bright at the center but faded into a pale blue at the edges, which blurred into the surrounding dark. Each lamp would glow until its chip was spent; once struck, mica had to burn itself out. It was not like a fire you could damp down or blow out to be relit later.

Jena looked around her, taking stock. Their progress had been painstakingly slow, but eventually the long stretch of tight tunnel had opened out into this cavernous space. Wide and accommodating at its base, it extended upward almost as far as the eye could see in a rapidly narrowing shaft. A thin stream of water trickled down it from somewhere far beyond sight, ending in a shallow pool at their feet. Asha and Kari sat nearby, sipping from their flasks.

Next to Jena, Renae lifted the last few flakes of mica from the patch in front of her. She tucked them into her pouch and then crawled over to join the others on the far side of the cavern, drawing a piece of dried fruit from her belt.

It was just Calla harvesting now, and Min. They were working alongside each other a few feet away. There had been no finger-touches today, no whispers into the darkness. When Jena directed Min to the center of the line behind Loren, she put her head down and followed without a sound. And when the rock opened out to reveal the mica's blue glow, she went immediately to her tools and set to work.

There was something hypnotic in the calm efficiency of her movements, and something familiar too: a sureness in the way she handled the knife.

Min turned her head. "I'm almost finished."

There were just a few last scrapes to be made, a final gentle levering of the mica that bloomed on the surface of the stone. There were veins through the rock wall here—deep-blue lines like those in an old Mother's legs—but they would not touch those. That harvest belonged to another line, another age.

"It's all right," Jena reassured her. "Don't hurry." She knelt beside her. "Did you see Berta yesterday?" In the confusion of this morning, she had forgotten to ask.

Min nodded. "Our bag . . . she added five scoops."

"Five?" Calla gave a low whistle. "That's more than we get."

"And how many in your house?" Jena asked softly.

It was not a question that called for a response, and Calla did not offer one. She tied her pouch at the neck, then moved over to join the others. Snippets of conversation floated across the cavern. Kari was telling stories about the baby while the others listened eagerly. "You should come and see her," she said. "All of you."

"Would they let us?" Asha asked.

The Mothers were understandably cautious with newborns. Family was one thing, but they could ill afford to endanger a daughter with the dirt from a hundred curious hands.

"Not likely," Renae said. "When Twila was born, they didn't let anyone visit for ages."

Asha looked thoughtful. "I would like to see her, though. Forty and forty."

"I know," Renae said. "Twila was forty-eight. I can't imagine a baby smaller than that."

"Thanks be." This last was a chorus of several voices, including Min's. She sheathed her knife and took her place on the edge of the group.

With the harvest secured, Jena allowed herself to relax. She sank to the floor of the chamber, feeling the cool of the stone seep through her thin garments. She drew her knees in to her chest and wrapped her arms around them, hugging herself close.

Min leaned across to Kari. "What did you say her name was?"

"Ailin."

"It's so pretty."

"Isn't it?" There were murmurs of agreement, but furtive glances at the rock too. None of them said what they were surely thinking. That it was early. Risky. No girl wanted to be the one to say such things out loud.

Instead, Min spoke again. "My name means precious. Thom says it's boring, but I like it."

"It's nice," Renae said. "Simple, but nice."

"Ralf is friends with your brother," Calla said.

"Not that one though—Ernst, I think."

"He's the eldest," Min said. "I've got five brothers. Thom's last, and then me."

"Five boys," Loren breathed. "I guess that's why you're precious. What were your numbers?"

"My numbers? I . . ."

"I'm sure they were better than mine," Calla said. "Fifty and forty-nine." She cast an appraising glance over her slender frame.

"Fifty's all right," Loren said.

Calla shook her head. "Not anymore."

Jena let their voices wash over her. Everyone liked talking numbers, but it could be a distraction in here. She knew she should keep the conversation in check, remind the girls to rest and drink, to breathe deeply and recover their strength.

But as she opened her mouth to do so, something occurred to her. Calla *Brandt.* Loren *Armen.*

Their family names had been on that paper along with Jena's. If she hadn't been interrupted, might she have found Asha's and Renae's there as well? And Kari's too?

No one was looking her way. She drew the paper from her pocket and rested it between her knees and chest, out of sight, angling her head lamp over the writing.

*Dietz.* Her heart raced as she made out the spidery writing near the bottom of the page. But just then Kari rose onto her haunches and called out across the cavern. "What are you doing, Jena?"

"Nothing." Jena lifted her head quickly, sending shafts of light bouncing off the stone.

"Is that a map? I thought you had it all in your head," Kari teased.

Jena crumpled the paper in her fist and shoved it back into her pants. "It's just rubbish. I must have left it in my pocket."

For a moment, she tried to believe her own words. That the paper was nothing. That it was just a page of old notes that had ended up in the back corner of the cupboard, alongside the bottle, by chance.

But she knew that it wasn't. This was the list of mamas who had been given that tonic. Tunneling mamas. Ripening early. Birthing tiny babies on the very edge of survival.

The Mothers were growing a line.

"Is something wrong?" Kari was looking at her oddly. Jena forced a smile, then reached for her water and took a long, slow swig, fighting to keep her hands from trembling.

She stood up. They had rested long enough. They

had been in the mountain long enough.

*Make the harvest. Find the light.* They were the Mothers' words, but today her reasons were her own.

"Get your gear. We're going."

Kari headed toward the opening in the rock.

"Not that way."

"But there's no other—"

"Yes, there is." Jena let the fading light from her lamp spill into the space overhead. There was a current of air there, the faintest waft of a familiar smell.

Signs, if you knew how to read them.

"Up there?"

"It will be quicker." Jena began to uncoil the rope.

Experience told her that before long the shaft would meet a wide fissure, an almost tunnel-like space sloping east-west. There were a few such passages in this part of the mountain, their walls smooth and accommodating, as if they had been hollowed out by the flow of rainfall or melting snow. If she was right, to go this way would save them hundreds of feet of slow, painstaking crawling.

She struck a fresh chip of mica and snapped it into her head lamp. After slipping the spent chip into a nearby crack, she reached through the opening, feeling for handholds. The sides of the shaft were jagged and rough, rocks jutting every which way. It was almost as if the mountain was giving them a ladder.

The others moved to the center of the cavern and roped in, falling into line behind her without a word.

It was the way, and so they took it.

# CHAPTER 13

Jena pulled herself into the shaft.

Hand over hand now, toe over toe. Below, the rope stretched taut, then slackened by turns as each girl followed.

As the space angled to the left, it narrowed briefly; it took Jena a minute to negotiate the bend, easing herself around the twisting contours of the rock. She paused just above and waited.

Asha grunted as she maneuvered herself through; it was some time before she emerged, rubbing a fresh graze on one elbow. She gave Jena a rueful look before perching alongside her on the opposite face of the shaft.

And now the others—*three . . . four . . .* Min passed through easily, Jena noted with satisfaction. Renae and Calla followed soon after, and there was only Kari to come.

Jena reached for the next handhold. Below, there was a pause, the sound of muffled voices, and then the rope found its rhythm once more.

Now it was just upward. Upward and out. Their progress was steady but laborious, and there were times when she came to a stop, waiting for the rope to slacken behind her so they could move on. She checked the impatience that rose in her at such times. It came harder to some; that was all. What mattered was that they got through.

Half an hour passed—perhaps more. They were close now; Jena could sense it. There was no smell or shift in the air this time, only the swinging of some internal compass. The shaft had risen far enough that they must be almost level with the wider passage. Just ahead, the way seemed to be opening out, spreading to make room.

It had been a tight climb, but this part at least would be easy. There was a bend here, but it too seemed wide, angling out like an elbow. And once they were clear of the shaft, there would be plenty of space around them. They could rest and stretch awhile, then push on. In a few short hours, they would be home.

But as Jena hauled herself around the bend, her eyes widened. It was a cruel trick. For the rock to open out like that only to constrict even farther than before, to close its throat upon them.

She had been right — the shaft came to an end here; just ahead she could see the point where it met one of the larger passages. But the way through was so narrow. A head's width? A hip's?

Jena glanced behind her — *beneath* her — to where the other girls waited. Could they descend from here, return the way they had come? Even with the lingering light from their head lamps, they would be climbing blind most of the time, their feet stepping down into space.

*Remember,* she scolded herself. What did she tell the others in training? *Trust the space.* Find a finger space and the hand will follow. And after that the arm. Ease yourself in. Ease yourself out. She edged forward. Breath held, ribs contracted. Head. Shoulders. Rock cut through the rough material of her shirt. Skin scraped and bled.

Hips. There was a moment then; fear knotted inside her, tight as a fist.

Something caught, then released. Legs followed arms. Lungs exhaled.

She was through.

She inched into the space, pulling up some slack in the rope, and then turned to look behind her. As her head lamp illuminated the gap through which she had come, she drew a sharp breath.

It was the narrowest opening, a bare sliver of space between two rocks. But this was what they trained for. She had passed through it, and the others would too.

"Come on," she urged. "It's fine."

Breath caught in throats. Stone etched itself into flesh. Between Asha and Loren, the rope frayed as it rubbed against a jagged rock. Once Loren was through, Asha drew her knife and cut the ragged strands from the rope. She took the two clean ends and tied them together, then pulled sharply, testing the knot.

*Three . . . four . . . five.* It was meaningless to count, but Jena did so anyway. As if her words might somehow help pull the others through.

They were six now, backs to stone, rubbing bruises, prodding scrapes, reminding themselves not to waste water on wounds. There was just Kari to come. Already Jena was looking around, testing the air. Which passage were they in? How much longer before they reached the outside?

She peered down the line. As each girl had emerged, Jena had shuffled farther away from the opening. The other girls' head lamps had dimmed almost to nothing, and she could only make out indistinct shapes in the gloom. She turned to Asha. "Is Kari through yet?"

Asha leaned away toward the others. Someone spoke, their voice muffled and blurry. Asha turned back to Jena. "She's coming. She's just—"

A cry echoed through the tunnel, ricocheting off the walls. It sounded eerie, distorted, but the voice was unmistakable.

*Kari.*

"What's happening?" Jena asked.

"I need more light." Calla's voice was quiet but steady.

"Here." Jena removed her own head lamp and passed it to Asha. She watched it move down the line to where Calla sat, bent almost double beneath the low stone roof. Calla shone the light into the opening, and Kari blinked as the glow hit her face. She was halfway through the opening, her torso flat to the floor of the tunnel, arms straining forward, fingers grasping. Her face was a sickly white.

"Jena." There was a deadening flatness in her voice. "I . . . I'm stuck."

"No, you're not. It's tight, that's all. Work the angles."

"I did. I have been." Kari's reply was clipped.

Kari knew as well as anyone what to do, how to turn and twist, to make herself small and fluid. But the others had come through. She must have missed something. It was like this sometimes—there was one precise passage and only one. You just had to find it, work yourself into it a certain way.

"One with the rock," Jena said. "Flatten and pull."

"I *know*!" Kari's voice cracked into a gulping sob.

Dread coiled inside Jena. This was the beginning of panic. She had seen it before—had watched it grow from a moment's weakness and then spiral on and on, feeding on itself until it was beyond any control.

Kari twisted, groaning, every movement labored, her breath coming in ragged gasps. "I *can't*, Jena." There was a new note in her voice, the sense of something rising to a point at which it must surely break.

Across the gloom of the tunnel, Jena's eyes met Calla's. She held her gaze until the other girl nodded, a sudden set to her jaw. Calla had not done this before—none of them had. But she knew what was needed. She passed the lamp to Renae and squared her shoulders.

Jena felt herself doing the same. What did it sound

like when a bone splintered? She forced back the nausea that threatened to overtake her.

"Take her hands," she said. "Pull."

Even as Calla began, Jena's mind tumbled with possibilities. If Kari broke — a hip, a leg? — they would have to get her out of the mountain somehow. Pushing, carrying, dragging.

Kari's scream cut across her thoughts. In the dim light, Calla's shoulders strained. There was another sound too. A muted sobbing.

*Min.* Jena felt a stab of disappointment; though this was a lot for a new tunneler to handle, she had such hopes for the girl. But then the light shifted and she saw that it was not Min but Renae, her shoulders shaking.

"Stop," Renae begged. "Please."

Jena opened her mouth to reply — to reassure Renae but to caution her too. While this was hard, it was necessary; they must not waver. But before she could speak, Min did so, her voice soft yet firm. "If you can't do it, then give it to me."

"It's just . . . what if . . . ?"

Without another word, Min leaned across Renae and took the lamp. "I've got it."

Renae slumped against the tunnel wall while Min

angled the light toward the opening. Calla began to pull once more, and Kari twisted, moaning.

Darkness clotted Jena's mind. Her hands clenched at her side.

There was a sound like something tearing, rending itself from the inside out. And then something was on her. Someone. It was dark and then light, shadows spinning wildly. Jena tumbled backward, throwing her hands out to break her fall. Asha was on top of her, and Loren upon Asha. The line collapsed onto itself as Calla staggered back, pulling the rope taut, and a body with it. In the mad kaleidoscope of light, Jena saw Kari's face—white, pitching forward into the tunnel.

"Kari?"

There was no answer, just a confusion of limbs. Girls struggled to right themselves, to disentangle. The light flickered, then steadied. The shadows stopped spinning, but still Jena couldn't see. The weight of the other girls was on her, and it took all the restraint she could summon not to push them away.

"Kari!" she repeated, more loudly this time.

"I'm out." The voice that answered was shaky, as though it were fighting for balance. "I'm—"

"You're hurt." It was Min who spoke. She lowered the lamp, tracking it along Kari's body. Loren leaned back, and Jena was finally able to see down the line. Kari was half-collapsed on the floor of the passage, arms outstretched, her hands still clutching Calla's. Her pants hung loosely in ragged strips where they had caught and shredded on the rock. She was bruised and bleeding. But none of that mattered.

"Are you broken?" Jena asked.

Kari hauled herself up onto her elbows, then her knees. She ran her hands down her sides, along her hips, her legs, gingerly at first, then more firmly.

"No," she said finally. "I think I'm okay. I . . ." She raised her head. "I'm sorry, Jena."

Jena gave a tight shake of her head. "It's not your fault."

Perhaps it was her own, for having led them this way, her thoughts upon her own purpose rather than that of the line, or the mountain. But that was not a question for now. Her eyes sought Kari's across the tunnel. "You're all right, then?"

In reply, Kari nodded sharply, her lips pressed together.

Jena motioned along the line. "Pass me the lamp."

Then she turned away down the tunnel and began to crawl.

❋

Deep in the mountain, Lia turns her head toward a sound.

It is muffled, distant, an echo coming to her through thick layers of stone. And so it cannot be what it sounds like, which is a voice, screaming.

Perhaps it is a skybird. Something outside, wheeling, calling.

Up ahead, there is a sliver of light, the edge of the sky leaking into the mountain. She had thought the village was at her back, but the fissures she has followed through the rock have led her up and down and every which way. Somewhere along the way, she must have gotten turned around. The mountain, she has learned, is full of such tricks.

She waits awhile, listening, but the sound does not come again.

*Home soon,* she tells herself. A fire in the hearth. Dinner. She must check her snare. Yesterday she lost track of time while she was in here and came out into darkness—too late to gather firewood, too late to catch the bird she had promised Father for the pot.

She must not let that happen again. It is one thing to come to the mountain; she must not neglect her chores on the outside.

She is turning back when she sees it. The smallest

shift in the light — a shadow slipping across it?

It must be a skybird. Not something to snare but to see — to watch quietly from a secret place, unobserved.

She will go home soon. Just not quite yet.

It is the slimmest crack in the stone, but it is enough. She turns toward it and begins to crawl.

# Chapter 14

Oh, it was high. Higher than Jena had expected.

They were above the canopy of the forest, looking down on the treetops. The sun had not yet crested the peaks of the mountain behind them; on the far side of the valley, the village was deep in shadow.

She leaned out, taking stock of the space, of their options. The sheer face of the mountain loomed from all sides—a sudden drop falling away below, the same rising above and around. There was no slope here, no convenient ladder of stone. There was nothing a girl could point to and say, *There is the way.*

But to go back? She shook her head. They were out now and must remain so. Kari was injured and had been close to panic; she needed to rest and heal. There were rocks here they could anchor to. Rocks that reached deep into the heart of the mountain, whose strength would secure their descent.

She took one end of the rope in the palm of her hand, feeling the fibers rub against her skin. Although they trained for it, they did not often descend like this. And it was rare for them to do so outside the mountain. Usually when they dropped a line, it was because a shaft had opened up beneath them, the harvest at its base and no way to get there but straight down.

"Are we going out?" It was Asha who spoke. The passage was wider here, and the girls had gathered just shy of the opening.

"Yes," Jena replied. "We'll go on the rope. But I want you in the middle, Kari. You can swap with Min."

It was a split-second decision but one that immediately felt right. Kari would feel more secure flanked by the others just now, and her injury meant she might need help starting her descent.

There was something else in it too, though—a reason Jena had not simply swapped the last two girls, directing Calla to bring up the rear. It was a way of telling Min that she had noticed—her calm, her steadiness; these things should be acknowledged and granted a certain kind of faith.

The girls untied themselves, and Jena secured the rope near the opening. Though the pull from their descent would make it impossible for the rope to slip upward, she nonetheless selected a tall rock that curved inward at the bottom. She drew the rope in tight at the base, tied an extra knot, and then another.

At this height, it didn't hurt to secure yourself against even the impossible.

Once the rope was in place, she fed it back through her legs and then up around her chest and shoulder. She wasted no time heading down, feet planted flat against the rock, one hand in front, gripping the rope, the other behind, feeding it through.

About a third of the way, she paused. Her lead foot had come away from the rock and was trailing in empty space. There was an overhang here—a point where the mountain sloped sharply back toward itself. But the angle was gentle enough, and with a little maneuvering, she was able to swing past and into the rock face below.

Before long, she was down, her toes reaching for ground. She stepped back and worked herself free from the rope, then looked beyond the edge of the overhang to where the others waited.

"All right!" she called, and immediately the rope

was drawn up the rock face, snaking back and forth as Asha positioned herself on it. A few minutes later, her legs swung over the ledge and she began the journey down.

Jena reached for the tail of the rope, taking the end in both hands. There was no way to act as a brake, but it felt wrong to let the rope dangle in space.

Loren followed Asha, and then it was Kari's turn. She took longer than the others, wincing as the rope fed along her injured side. Her tattered pants hung loose, and though she had gathered them around her as best she could, Jena could see that her leg was bloodied and torn; even the skin that remained was purpling into mottled bruises.

Still, Kari descended smoothly and did not cry out; it wasn't long before she stood beside Jena on the ground, breathing heavily. She motioned to the rope. "Do you want me to hold it?"

"Just rest." Jena pointed to where Asha and Loren had settled on the fringe of the forest, their backs against tree trunks. As Kari joined them, Jena turned her attention back to the rope — to Renae, then Calla, and finally, Min.

Min came down as deftly as if she had done this every day of her life. The rhythm of her hands on the rope, the ease with which her body folded into and out of itself.

She had done so well today, better than anyone might have hoped. Jena resolved to tell her so on the way back; she would take her aside, let the others walk ahead for a time.

Her mind was on this when the rope jerked in her hand.

Her fingers closed reflexively around it, or tried to. It whipped erratically, as if it had been caught in a sudden storm.

"Min?" The sun was cresting the top of the mountain just above, darts of light shooting through the narrow spaces between the peaks. It was blinding, the sudden bright force of it hurting her eyes. It took an act of will to continue to stare into it, but she did so, straining to make out the shape of the girl.

The rope had stilled and Jena took up the end again, feeling herself exhale. Above, in the wash of light, Min seemed to have stopped. She was at the lip of the overhang, poised on the rope.

There was a slight movement, and Min leaned in toward the face of the mountain. Perhaps she was troubled by the overhang, trying to find the best way past. "It's all right," Jena called. "It's easy. Just—"

There was no sound. No scream. The rope was yanked from her hand, searing heat against her palms. Going and then gone.

For a moment, pure stillness. The valley held its breath.

Then let it go.

Clouds in front of the sun. A shape becoming clear. Hands flailing, feet kicking, holding on to nothing. A figure, freewheeling in the sky. The rope unraveling around Min as she tumbled, as she fell.

Clear of the rope now, stumbling, as if she were searching for a foothold in the air.

It seemed slow but must have been quick. So quick. Behind Jena, someone screamed.

*Min!*

Jena's hands grabbed pointlessly for the rope.

*Make yourself limp. Be soft upon the ground.*

The Mothers' words spun through her head, useless.

Oh. It was high. Higher than she had expected.

Oh. It was a long way to fall.

✳

It is not her fault.

Lia tells herself this, but she does not believe it.

When she presses her face to the crack, she sees not a skybird but a girl. A small white face, neat black hair, lively eyes darting.

The girl does not notice her at first. And why would she? There is so much for her to see out there in the sky. She must have a view of the whole village from here, and more. The great flat of the land stretching all the way to the coastline and beyond. The dazzling blue of the sea.

She is an odd-looking girl, but Lia would like to know her. Because if she is up here on the rock, she is a girl who likes secret places, who wants to see for herself no matter what people say. Perhaps the kind of girl who might be a friend.

So Lia speaks, softly at first. "Hello?"

And when the girl looks around, startled, then shakes her head as if to knock loose some ridiculous idea that has crept inside, she tries again, more loudly.

"Hello!" And manages now to wedge her fingers through the crack a little lower down, so her hand is reaching out—just slightly.

The girl's eyes widen; her lips part. Her pale face jerks to one side. She is swinging somehow. There is a rope, and her hands are on it and then they are not.

Fingertips brush Lia's for one fragile heartbeat, and then they are gone.

The girl's eyes are all surprise as she falls backward, reaching, scrambling, her hands closing over and over on nothing but air.

And then she is gone.

Far below, the sound of screaming. No way to think this a bird.

It is not her fault, Lia tells herself. But, oh, she does not believe it.

# CHAPTER 15

They put Min in the ground under a cloudless sky.

Her brothers formed a ragged line, their mama and papa between them, the Mothers behind, heads bowed. Jena stood to one side, flanked by the other girls. Kari's hand slipped into hers, squeezed.

As the earth closed above Min, her mama stepped forward, hands clenched at her sides. A sob escaped her throat, and her knees seemed about to buckle. But then she straightened and turned back to those who had gathered in the clearing.

It was almost the whole village. There was no time at this end of the season—no time for anything but the chopping of wood and the laying in of stores—but still they had come.

"She was a good girl," her mama said. "She worked hard."

You could see the daughter in the mama, Jena thought. Something about the shape of the nose, the jaw. The neat, compact lines of her body.

Unbidden, the image of that small figure flashed in front of her, the crumpled bundle at her feet.

Time had seemed to stop. There was a moment when she felt that if she could just take a step back, she might unstitch something, reverse it. That there must be something she could do to put this right.

Her burning hand, reaching for the girl. The soft head, the downy fuzz at the nape of her neck suddenly unbearable. She thought of Ailin, of what was ahead. Of Min, and what was behind. All those years—wrapping, training, hoping. The barest handful of harvests. This.

Min's mama turned to the Mothers. "It is the way, I know. I do not question it. But—"

There was a cry from one of Min's brothers, a raw sound like an animal might make.

*Thom.* All at once, Jena was inside the mountain again, snug against the stone while the girls' easy banter ricocheted around her. *Precious.* She bit her lip, gripped Kari's fingers hard.

Mother Berta placed an arm around Min's mama,

drawing her into the folds of her cloak. "It is a great sadness," she said. "But it is the way."

Beside her, Mother Vera held up a hand. As one, the crowd stilled, waiting. They had come to farewell a daughter, but they had come for this too. To hear the reason, to make sense of it.

When tragedy struck the line, there was always a reason. It meant the mountain had something to teach them, a message they needed to hear. But the village had never lost a daughter like this. If the mountain took a girl, it did so inside. It kept her, holding her deep within its heart. It did not throw her off like a creature swatting an insect from its hide.

There was a message here, but they could not divine it. That was the work of the Mothers, who spoke the language of the rock, whose ancestors had emerged impossibly from its crevices. Yesterday, they had spoken with the girls of the line, each one in turn, and then quietly among themselves. They had visited the mountain, had sat in its shadow, contemplating the point where the rope hung slack at its side.

The rope had not broken. It had not snapped or frayed. Min had simply fallen, dropping soundlessly to the earth as swiftly and cleanly as a bird felled by an arrow midflight.

Vera began speaking, her reedy voice cutting through the crisp morning air. "We should not tie ourselves to the rock. Nor indeed one to the other." She looked out across the gathered faces. "We go in as seven, and it is the mountain that binds us. It was the way of the first Seven. It should be our way too."

Voices swirled around Jena, uncertain. Berta's eyes met her own, and now the old Mother stood alongside Vera. "We need nothing so crude as rope. We must trust."

That level gaze, calm and reassuring, blanketing the crowd.

*Of course. How did we not see this?* The voices were soft at first, then rose to a hum, the crowd seeming to form a single voice.

The Mothers' words hung in the air. Kari's hand was suddenly clammy in Jena's.

The rope. It had been part of their training from the very beginning. *Through the loops, like so. Check the knots. Again.*

"The rock cut one rope," Vera went on, "and we did not listen. We thought we knew better."

Jena shot a glance at Asha. Her face was red and blotchy, her eyes downcast.

"We angered the mountain and it shrugged our

daughter off," Berta said. "We will not make the same mistake again. We learn from the past so as not to repeat it." She turned to Min's mama. "It is an important lesson. Thank you for giving us your daughter so we might learn it."

"Thank you," the Mothers echoed.

Berta reached into her cloak and withdrew something, held it aloft. Then she took the woman's hand. "A stone for your daughter." She pressed it into the opened palm, closed the fingers over it as you might those of a child.

Min's mama knelt beside the mound of earth.

*Thank you.* The refrain was taken up by voices in the crowd.

Thom stood on the other side of Min's mama. He was so slight, so pale. There was a brother at each shoulder, as if they were securing him between them, holding him up. Luka was nearby, on the edge of the family. His lips were unmoving, his mouth set in a thin line.

"Jena." Asha's voice was in Jena's ear. "I'm sorry about the rope. I didn't think. I . . ."

"It's not your fault."

"I should have listened. I didn't realize."

"None of us did." Her reply was sharper than she

had intended. There was an unease gnawing at her, something shadowy taking shape on the edge of her thoughts.

The mountain had not seemed angry. The day—the rock—had been calm around them. A rope had frayed on a sharp stone, but that was not so strange. Once or twice a season such a thing might happen. When it did, they simply cut and retied, continued on their way.

As the mourners began to disperse, Jena let the crowd flow past like the waters of the spring around a log. The ground above Min's grave was raw, fresh as a wound.

She looked beyond to where her mama lay. In the long grass, the glass from the bottle glinted as a wan sunbeam struggled through the leafy canopy. Tears pricked the corners of Jena's eyes, blurring the light. From here, Mama was little more than a ripple on the grassy surface. The earth had sealed over her, leaving no trace.

*Except for me,* Jena thought. *I am her trace.*

*If there is no one left to speak for her, it has to be me.*

Her hand slipped from Kari's and into her pocket, closing tightly around the paper. There was a message here. She would learn how to read it.

# Chapter 16

"Jena!" The voice that called through the trees was half shout, half whisper.

Kari had gone ahead to visit Ailin, and Jena was on her way back to the village. She had chosen a roundabout path, hoping to avoid conversation, but now Luka appeared, beckoning.

"In here. I need to talk to you."

There was something pleading in his eyes. She turned off the path with a sigh.

Luka pressed a finger to his lips. He began to walk deeper into the forest, motioning for her to follow. The undergrowth was not as thick as elsewhere, and when they came to a stop a few minutes later, Jena realized why. There was a path here once, though it had not been used for many years.

This was the place she and Kari used to call the skeleton houses—the quarrying huts in which their ancestors had sheltered after Rockfall, thinking it would not be long before they found a way out or rescue came from the other side. In a way, this was where the village had begun. Above, the canopy of trees was thick enough that hardly any light penetrated. From here, you could almost believe there was no such thing as sky.

Jena shivered. As a child, she'd had nightmares about the ruined frames sunk deep in forest, the old timber collapsed upon itself like crumbling ribs.

Luka sat heavily on the ground near a curtain of creeping rag-vine, wedging his back against the corner of what might once have been a wall. Jena settled opposite on a rotting beam; it was half sunk in dirt, as if it were returning to the earth.

"It's Thom," Luka said. "I have to do something. I can't just let them freeze."

Jena met his eyes. "They've been doing this for a long time, Luka. They'll find a way." She did not speak the dark thought that slunk into her mind. That if nothing else they had one fewer mouth to feed.

"How can they?" Luka's voice cut across the stillness of the forest. "Seven of them? On three scoops of mica?"

"Three? But . . ." Jena's skin was suddenly cold. With Min gone, her allocation would be too. Five sons, a broken mama, a winter fast approaching. "The Mothers won't do that. They can't." Her fingers fidgeted at the edge of the beam beneath her. The fragile wood crumbled at the lightest touch.

"They already have. I heard them talking last night. They left an extra half scoop, for the lesson." Luka snorted. *"Thank you for giving us your daughter so we might learn it."* He stared at Jena, as if challenging her to argue. "We have to get him some."

"But we can't. I—"

"I thought of taking some from ours, but Berta . . . she's too careful. Everyone is. No one will give any up, and they'll notice if it's gone."

"But it's the same for the pouches," Jena said. "The girls know what they've harvested. There's no way I could—"

"I didn't mean that. I thought . . . maybe you could go in."

"On my own?"

Luka flushed. "I just thought there might be some way."

"It's not that simple, Luka. I'd have to go deep. People would notice I was gone." Jena broke a splinter of wood from the beam and traced a thin line in the dirt. "I can't just—"

"All right." Luka's voice was clipped. "Forget I asked." He reached up and pulled a tendril of vine down toward him. He did not break it from the plant but began coiling the end around one leg. The vine seemed endless; it straightened as he pulled, dragging more with it, and before long his leg was a mass of dark-green fibers.

He gave a wry smile. "Maybe if I wrap this tightly enough, I can go in myself."

Jena felt something in her loosen. With everything Luka had been saying, he seemed less like Berta's grandson and more like her friend.

She bent the wood between her fingers, snapping it in half. "I want to show you something." She reached into her pocket and withdrew the crumpled piece of paper, then pressed it into the palm of his hand.

He smoothed the paper out across his knees as she had done in the mountain. "What is this?"

Jena explained—about the smell, the broken bottle, Min's mama, the ledgers. And what Luka himself had said, that night at the feast.

"But that doesn't mean anything. The Mothers . . . they know things. Things other people can't see. The same way . . ." He groped for words. "The same way you know the rock. There might have been signs."

Jena shook her head. "The ledger said *ripen.* That's something you do . . . something *they did.*"

"And this was there?"

"It was with the bottle. It's the names of all the mamas they've given it to. And that's the dosage." She plucked the paper from his lap and pointed at the tiny notations scribbled alongside each name. "See how it changes a bit each time? And the names . . . they're all tunneling mamas."

A deep furrow creased Luka's brow. "You think they're doing it for the *line*?"

"I know it's hard to believe, but . . ."

"Forty and forty," Luka breathed. He traced the words with the tip of one finger, like they were something he might read by touch. "But didn't you say Thom's mama had it too?"

"That was different. They weren't trying to . . . *ripen* her." The word was bitter in Jena's mouth. "Min said the baby had died; the tonic was just to help get it out."

"But what about Min? She was in the line. If you're right, wouldn't her mama have had it, then?"

"I thought about that. But then I realized . . . Renae's mama isn't there either."

"So?"

"They were never in the line. Their mamas . . . they're not tunneling families. Min only has brothers. Renae's sister works in the bakery."

Jena watched as understanding grew on Luka's face. It had taken her a while to make sense of it herself. The Mothers were careful. They knew what they were doing was risky, so they only chose certain mamas for the tonic—those who had tunneled themselves and whose daughters were most likely to do the same.

Daughters who came earlier and smaller, *if the rock allowed it.* Seven moons? Six?

*Thanks be.*

But sometimes they got it wrong. Sometimes a mama's fragile body simply broke under the strain.

Sometimes they put a mama in the ground and then added a spidery note. *Too strong. Reduce dosage.*

Luka's eyes widened. "Berta said the mountain was showing us favor."

Jena did not reply.

"She said that's why daughters were getting smaller. She . . ." He trailed off. "What are we going to do?"

"I don't know." Whenever Jena tried to think past what she had learned, she hit a wall as sheer and as steep as the face of the mountain itself.

"Let me see what I can find out," Luka said finally. "I can ask her things."

Jena hesitated.

"Don't worry. I'll be careful."

She considered for a moment, then held out the paper. "Take this."

As Luka reached for it, there was a sound in the nearby undergrowth. The rustling of dry leaves, a thin branch bending and then snapping back into position. He rose awkwardly, wincing as the vine tightened around his leg. "What's that?"

Jena turned toward the sound. It was late in the morning for a rabbit, but there was definitely something. It was low to the ground, a dirty brown color flashing through the spaces between the leaves. There was a scrabbling sound, and the bushes heaved on either side.

Wings?

"A landbird?" Luka whispered. "It can't be."

Jena held her breath. But as the creature flapped wildly, sending leaves flying up around it, she saw there was something haphazard, lopsided, about its movements.

This was not a landbird running madly through the undergrowth but a skybird—trying to take off.

"There." Jena pointed as it broke clear of the bushes. But Luka was already moving, circling behind the bird in a wide loop.

"We can get it!" He stripped the vine from his leg and motioned to Jena. "Go around that side."

The bird was between them now, but Jena was closer. She tiptoed toward it, placing her feet carefully to avoid sudden noise. Still the bird turned, as if guided by some inner sense. Its wings came up again, and at the same time Jena reached down, folding them back onto its body, gathering the bird between her hands. Beneath her palms, she felt the wings trying to beat, but she resisted, holding them firm against its sides.

"Plenty of meat on it." Luka picked up a stone from the ground nearby.

Jena looked down at the bird. The edge of one wing was folded slightly back onto itself, but there was no other sign of injury. Was this all it took to bring a creature low?

She held the bird and Luka held the stone. They regarded each other silently.

He had wanted her to catch it and she had. But now it was here, its warm body trembling in her hands. And it seemed impossible to think on what should come next.

She had seen dead birds before, broken skybirds with arrows in their sides or their necks bent at awkward angles. The hunters brought them back, slung across their chests or between poles with their feet tied together, glassy eyes staring, slackened beaks gaping.

But this was nothing like that. The bird pulsed with life, straining upward. When Jena relaxed her grip, the bent wing began to straighten and extend. Perhaps all it had needed was to be clear of the undergrowth. Perhaps it was simply a thing that had lost its way, its family. That might find them again if given the chance.

Luka did not raise his hand. "We could take it back. I could carry it."

Jena considered. The Mothers would be glad of it. They would keep it in a cage behind the Stores to fatten it up, then cook it fresh for a feast.

Someone would kill it, but it wouldn't be them.

Did that change things, even a little?

The bird turned its head, seeming to fix a beady eye upon Jena. She looked at Luka, and something unspoken passed between them. He let the stone fall to the ground at his feet.

Jena held the bird against her chest, cupping her

hands beneath its wings, freeing them. They began to flap immediately, reaching out. It was chaotic at first, all struggle and no symmetry. She held fast and waited, and before long the wings began to beat together, finding a rhythm.

She raised the bird aloft — head height and then beyond, as high as she could manage. Then released.

It began as a kind of staggering motion, as if the bird were trying to grasp something, scrambling for an invisible handhold. Jena held her breath, hoping, willing it on. And then the wind flared beneath it, and it seemed to mount the air, lifting up and up. It reached the canopy and Jena thought, *oh,* for the branches were thick with leaves and there was no way through.

But as she thought this, the bird gave a flick of its tail and pushed higher, and she saw that there was a space — were spaces — after all. That there had been all along, if you were a bird.

And if you were not — if you were a girl, feet held fast to earth — you could at least follow its passage, stand below and watch as it went through, turning this way and then that, like an old Mother threading the finest of needles.

Luka stood beside Jena, his neck craned skyward. They watched as the bird disappeared, until the only sign it had been there at all was the quivering of branches, a handful of leaves falling quietly to the forest floor around them.

There was no need for either to say what they were thinking. They had done a wrong thing, a right thing.

They would tell no one, ever.

✳

*She will tell no one, ever.*

*Papa has been unwrapping her. Jena is five, and she has to keep to the schedule. But at bedtime Papa says,* What can it hurt? *and* Who will know? *And when the last of the wrappings falls to the floor, he breathes out as though he is the one being released and says,* There. Isn't that better?

*Jena cannot answer. Though there is no girl who doesn't long for this sometimes, it is not better. It is easier; it is more comfortable. But that is not the same thing. A girl unwrapped will never make the line.*

*When Papa leaves, he takes the wrappings with him, and so she pulls her blankets tight around her. This will do for now, and soon enough it will not matter because she will be at the Center. The Mothers said she is to spend the winter there with the little ones. Five is too old for that, but she doesn't mind. She will be with her sister, and when spring comes, the old Papa will* be back. All he needs is time, the Mothers said, and winter will give him that.

The baby will grow over the winter. Already she is changing. When she is unwrapped, she reaches for things—a hand, a face. When she is wrapped, she tilts herself from side to side, as if she were trying to roll, to tip herself over.

Seeing this makes Jena feel strange, puts an itching in her limbs. And when the baby's forehead knots in frustration, she feels her own do the same.

When the baby cries, Jena sits at her bedside. I know, she croons. I know.

It is hard when you are little and cannot understand. When you do not know about the mountain and the line.

One day you will see, she thinks. One day I will tell you.

But for now, she strokes and soothes, and soon enough her sister falls asleep and is still.

At home, there is no one to soothe Jena. She lies in bed awake.

Down the darkened hall, a door clicks. Footsteps pad nearby and voices drift across the night.

It is something she once loved—the sleepy sound of Mama and Papa, their soft voices murmuring while her eyelids became heavier, sinking toward sleep.

But there is no Mama now, and Papa's voice is different. It

sounds cracked, as if someone has taken an ax and split it open.

Trust them?

*Another voice, gentler.* Darius, we must.

*Her door is closed, but light leaks in underneath. It is late. She knows this because the moon is high overhead, and she knows this because slivers of white light slice through the roof timbers, making ghostly fingers upon the walls and the floor.*

*Three stripes of moonbeam on her bed means three too-large gaps. Means corridors through which winter might reach its icy fingers.*

*She told Papa about them last week, but he said,* Hush, child. Not now. *And looked past her, as if he were seeking a point far in the distance.*

*It is too bright to sleep. The moon is on her face, pale and cold.*

*The voices down the hall rise and fall. It is late for voices, especially this loud. Even the soft voice is louder now, and she knows who it is. It is Uncle Dietz, and this is lucky because he is good with roofs, like Papa.*

*She pushes back the blankets and swings her legs out onto the coarse matting.*

*She will tell Uncle Dietz about the moonlight, about the cold. He will listen and say she is good and helpful. And tomorrow he will put on his belt and climb up with his hammer and his nails and he will fix things.*

*At the end of the hall, she hesitates. She will wait her turn because that is what big girls do when other people are talking, and that is what is happening now. The kitchen door is ajar, and words upon words are spilling from it, fast and blurry.*

I can't, Karl. Could you?

You have to. What else can we —

Something. I don't know. There has to be something.

It is the way, Darius. You know that. It —

How can it be the way? *Papa is shouting now.* Look at what it does to them! My Clara. And Jena . . . it's all she wants. She will follow her mama and . . . I can't let them, Karl. I —

*And then there is a sound — something falling, shattering?*

*She pushes the door open. The light is suddenly bright and Papa is there in the middle of it. His fist is on the table. On the floor, pieces of a bowl lie broken, sharp-edged. Uncle Dietz is half sitting, half standing.*

I'm sorry, Darius. I just meant —

I know what you meant.

*There is something brittle in Papa's voice. The way his whole body seems clenched, the something wild in his eyes. It is almost not Papa.*

*Everything here is wrong. Papa and Uncle Dietz stare at each other, wary, as if the space between them is too great to cross.*

*Papa? Jena steps into the kitchen. When he sees her, something changes in Papa's face.*

Jena? What are you doing up?

I can't sleep.

We woke you, *Uncle Dietz says.* I'm sorry. *Then he leans down, frowning.* Why aren't you wrapped? *He turns to Papa.* Darius?

*Jena tugs his sleeve, turns him back to her.* I'm off tonight. The Mothers said.

But Kari . . .

She's four, *Jena says.* I'm five.

Of course. *Uncle Dietz scoops her up.* Come on, then. Let me put you back.

*She is flopped over his shoulder, and they are halfway down the hall. Papa stands in the open door of the kitchen, one hand raised in a funny little wave.*

*As they step through her doorway, Jena raises her own in reply.*

*She is five. And that is old enough to know that some things are secrets.*

*He has grown strange to her. But he is Papa. So she will tell no one.*

# CHAPTER 17

"That one?" Mother Anya pointed at a dark shape easing its way through the slats of the maze.

She was flanked by several other Mothers. Their shrewd gazes darted back and forth as a series of girls took their turn in the narrow passages. Just a few remained inside now; a handful lurked nearby, their faces downcast.

After letting the bird go, Jena and Luka had separated in the forest. While he headed for the Square, she skirted the base of the mountain to the back of the village, thinking she might slip home quietly. But as she rounded the last corner, she realized her mistake. A crowd had gathered at the maze. It was crawling with girls, their eyes shining.

In the long shadow of the rock, their families, fresh from a funeral, stood willing them on.

When they saw Jena, they called to her. *My daughter . . . you must see her. My girl . . . she was forty-eight, forty-nine.*

And then the Mothers beckoned her over. To watch, to help choose.

The girl Anya had indicated reached an open part of the maze. An arm protruded first, followed by a fair head. She might have been nine, Jena thought, though it was always hard to tell.

Berta turned to Jena. "What do you think?"

Jena could not bring herself to reply. Although she had done this before, today was different. Standing here, she felt like a hunter sizing up a bird or a rabbit. Which to take, and which to leave for another day?

Someone had looked at her in this way once. How eager she had been. Just like these girls. And Kari too. Both of them waiting, hoping for their chance.

"Child?"

Jena bobbed her head in assent. The Mothers would make their choice in any case. Soon enough there would be a new girl behind her, the line replenished.

Anya motioned to the girl to exit, and she pulled herself clear, her face split in a broad grin.

"And the other?"

"I'm not sure. Maybe the tall one?"

The Mothers muttered among themselves. Perhaps, Jena thought, they had not yet chosen but were narrowing it to two. Perhaps there would be some final test.

But the fair girl had reached them now, and Berta bent down, congratulating her. "Come to the Stores later. We'll get you some gear."

The girl spoke, suddenly bold. "My friend Marla . . . we always train together. She had trouble before, but she's really good. She—"

"Child." Berta silenced her with a word. "It is not for you to speak."

The girl flushed, chastened.

"I don't understand," Jena said. "Are we to take another?"

It couldn't be. The thought of going in with eight was absurd. Anya stared at Jena, an odd expression on her face. "Has no one told you?"

"Told me what? I don't—"

It was Berta who replied, her voice gentle. "Kari is thickening, child." Her forehead creased into deep ridges. "I thought she would have spoken with you."

The air around Jena suddenly felt too heavy to breathe. "No. She can't be. She . . ." Disbelief gave ground suddenly to something else. Kari's face swam in front of her eyes, white in the lamplight. *I'm stuck. I'm sorry.*

Berta sighed. "We all walk a different path. It is the mountain that decides."

"In this, as in all things." The words rolled unbidden from Jena's tongue.

"Just so, child." The Mother's response faded behind her as Jena turned on her heel and hurried away.

✷

Kari was perched on a stool beside Ailin's crib. When she saw the look on Jena's face, she lowered her eyes.

"Why didn't you tell me?" There was something in her own voice Jena couldn't quite recognize. Was it anger she felt? Disappointment, perhaps. Sadness.

But there was something stronger too. A feeling that buzzed beneath the surface of her skin.

"I'm sorry," Kari said simply. "I hoped I wouldn't have to. I thought maybe I could stop it."

"How long have you known?"

"A few months, maybe. At first I thought my wrappings had shrunk." She pinched at the skin around her waist. "I thought if I was more careful . . ."

Jena cast her mind back. Kari skipping breakfast. *I'm going to help with Ailin. I'll eat later.* Pushing her dinner plate across the table. *I'm all right. I ate earlier.*

Kari leaned over the crib. "Mama noticed too. She said she thickened at my age, so she's been keeping an eye on me. She hoped I might have longer. But . . ." She shrugged. "I went to Mother Marla, to see if—"

"Kari, no," Jena gasped. Like Dyan, Mother Marla was a healer. But unlike Dyan, she was responsible for more than tonics and remedies. If you broke a bone, she would set it for you. And if a bone needed breaking, if a girl needed adjusting, then . . .

"You don't have to worry. She said it's too late." Kari poked a hand through the wooden slats of the crib. "It's all right, Jena. I don't mind. You were always better than me anyway." Her voice was flat, but her face seemed to lighten while she spoke, as if doing so unburdened her. "Just like our mamas. We all walk a different path. And we'll be okay. We have your allocation and Ailin coming through. And I'll still get some." She gave a shy smile. "Berta said I need to look after myself, stay strong. Maybe one day I'll get to be a mama too." Her fingers trailed lightly across Ailin's cheek. "Meanwhile, I have to find something else to do. Renae's mama said she could use someone at the bakery. Maybe I'll learn to make bread or something."

She let out a soft peal of laughter. Her eyes met Jena's, inviting her to join in. Instead, Jena gripped the edge of the crib, her mind reeling.

What Kari said was true. Soon enough it would be her turn to birth a daughter. To swallow a tonic—for strength or healing or who knows what.

*Just like our mamas.*

The words sent a chill through Jena. What else would they repeat?

Mama. Papa. Min.

*Observe the loss; fly on.*

Ailin was waking. Tiny undulations rippled her wrappings as she stretched beneath them. She tensed her shoulders, straining outward, her face reddening with the effort.

Kari wrinkled her nose. "She'll need changing."

Jena reached down into the crib.

"Not yet. She'll feed first."

"It's not that." Jena's fingers probed for the end of the wrappings.

"What are you doing?"

"It's too tight. I need to—"

"Stop it!" Kari's whisper echoed in the stillness of the room. She put a hand on Jena's arm. "You can't."

Ailin began to cry, and Irina's dark head appeared at the door. "Awake already?"

Jena slumped back.

"I'll get her milk," Irina called.

Kari exhaled heavily but did not relax her grip. "Jena, what's wrong?"

"I don't know. I . . ." Jena had spoken without a sense of what would come next, and now it was as if the path she had begun to lay had petered out in front of her.

"That . . . it's what your papa used to say. It's what he used to do." There was a tremor in Kari's voice.

"I know. I remember."

"No, you don't. I only know because Papa said so." Kari hesitated. "He and Mama . . . they talk sometimes."

"I do remember." All at once Jena felt that she might look up and see Papa—charging in, arguing, his strong arms reaching. Before, memories had been distant things that had to be dredged up. Now they seemed to swim just below the surface of her thoughts, ready to break through at any moment. "I remember what it was like, Kari. All those hours. Didn't we—?"

"You don't have to tell me," Kari said quickly. "It's hard at first; everyone knows that."

"Do you ever think," Jena said tentatively, "that things could be different? That maybe there's another way?"

"Jena, no." Color drained from Kari's face. "Your papa . . . it was because of your mama. You know that. Papa said he just got too sad." Her hold on Jena's arm relaxed; her fingers became caresses, curling softly on Jena's skin. "I can't imagine what that was like. What it *is* like. If I lost Mama, I . . . we're just so glad you turned back. That we didn't lose you too." Kari reached for Ailin and picked her up, clasping her close against her chest.

"We're family," she said. "I'm sorry I didn't tell you. And I'm sorry we can't tunnel together anymore. I'm going to miss it. A lot. I can't really think about it too much. It's so strange." She sighed. "But that's the only thing that's changing. Everything else is going to stay just the way it is."

Kari could not have known Jena found no comfort in her words.

Ailin began to fuss. Her mouth gummed at Kari's chest, bobbing up and down like a bird pecking at the ground. Jena glanced at the downy head, then turned away. She could not bear to think of those fragile plates.

Instead, she called up the image of the bird she and Luka had found. Had saved. Where would it be now? Perched high on the mountain, perhaps, gazing down on them all. Or curled in a nest somewhere, sheltered and still.

But when she closed her eyes, all she could see was its upward spiral as it beat higher and higher, disappearing finally through that impossible hole.

✳

*Jena is five. Yes, five. Papa still hasn't remembered, but she doesn't mind because something exciting is happening, something that has shaken the numbers clear out of her head.*

*There is no bird, but Papa has packed some dried fruit and bread.* Supplies, *he calls it,* for the journey.

*There is no birthday doll, but there is something more wonderful. There is a baby—a tiny sister cradled in Papa's arms, and perhaps later, if Jena is good and quiet, he will let her hold her.*

*When he does, she will hold her close. She will fold her arms and legs tight against her body, because that is what babies like.*

It is what babies need, and Jena doesn't know why Papa has unwrapped her. As they walk, her dangling limbs flail and her cries ring out across the darkening night.

But Papa won't listen when Jena tries to tell him. He just says, Shh, shh! — to her and to the baby both — and quickens his pace.

He seems different, though, and that is good. He is gentle again, his eyes almost smiling.

Jena was asleep when he came. There were no voices tonight and no moonbeams. Uncle Dietz has fixed the gaps. Even though Jena is five, he would not let her come on the roof. It was too dangerous, he said, for her special bones. But he let her choose the wood and pass him the hammer.

When he had finished, he ruffled her hair and said she was an excellent helper. And then he lowered his face to hers and said, Be patient with your papa. It is hard for him. And for you too, I know.

Jena has been patient, and now, tonight, it is like old Papa is back. His voice was soft when he called her, when he shook her shoulder gently, saying, Wake up, Jena. It's time to go. As they hurry through the empty streets, his steps are light.

They do not pass through the Square but keep to the edge of the village, skirting the rocky paths behind the houses at the very back. And when they reach the long street that leads out toward the fields and the forest, Jena wonders why they have come this way at all. The other is so much faster. It is the way they always go.

This is a journey, but it is not one she understands.

Something wicked is happening, and something wonderful. They are the same thing, somehow, and that makes no sense. She cannot get any of it straight in her mind.

She is five. She repeats it with every footstep. Five, five, five.

Is it old enough, she wonders as they cross the fields and enter the inky thicket of forest, to ask Papa what he is doing, where they are going? To say, Wait, Papa, stop.

It is not. And so she doesn't.

There is nothing to do but follow.

And so she does.

# CHAPTER 18

Jena lay awake in the darkness. Nearby, Kari's breathing rose and fell, making its own steady rhythm.

For a time, they had been awake together but silent. It was as if something were balanced between them, waiting for one of them to pluck it. Eventually, Jena heard Kari roll over, but whether it was toward her or away, she couldn't have said.

At dinner, Mama Dietz had slipped Kari an extra helping of stew. She did it quietly, but Jena noticed all the same. Kari glanced quickly at Jena, something new in her eyes.

Now Jena's gaze lingered on the dark shape in the other bed. Although Kari was right there, it felt like she had left, had gone on ahead to a place where Jena couldn't follow.

She rolled toward the wall, pulling the blankets tightly around her. And then came a sound. It was a kind of tapping—soft at first but then louder, insistent. And with it a voice, low and urgent.

"Jena!"

She sat up and peered out the window.

"Get up! I need you to come outside."

"Shh!" Jena glanced over at Kari. She swung her feet onto the floor, then padded out into the hall, pulling the door closed gently behind her.

Luka had come around to the front door. He jiggled on the balls of his feet, his face pale.

"What is it?" Jena asked. "I—"

Luka was panting, out of breath. Instead of replying, he raised a hand and pointed—across the rooftops and out at the forest. Jena squinted, then stepped outside to stand alongside him.

The air around them was cold, the night crisp and sharp-edged. The village was sunk in darkness, every light long extinguished. Above, the night sky was seeded with stars.

It was peaceful. Soothing, almost. And then she saw what Luka was pointing at. Above the tree line on the far side of the forest, a figure was silhouetted against the rock in a pale wash of moonlight. From here, it appeared to be suspended in midair, but Jena knew what anchored it to the mountain's side.

The rope, left to hang where she had fixed it — as a reminder, as a warning.

A slight figure making its way slowly upward.

"Thom?" Jena's hand flew to her mouth. Her fingers fluttered, then curled into a fist. She turned back to Luka. "What's he doing?"

"I don't know. I thought he was going to the graveyard. I went after him to see if he was okay, but then . . ." He waved wildly at the mountain. "He won't listen to me. You have to come."

✳

"Thom, stop!"

Jena could not keep pace with Luka, and he was out of sight when she heard him call. By the time she broke clear of the trees, he was at the foot of the rope. Thom had almost reached the top; another few feet would put him at the opening.

"You have to come down." Luka's voice was quieter this time, but still loud enough to carry to where Thom hung, his feet planted flat on the rock.

There was no reply, but Jena saw Thom's shoulders

slump. He began to sob, great gulping cries that echoed off the stone.

"Thom?" she called tentatively. "I don't know what you're doing, but—"

"It's my fault." Thom's body shook, making the rope swing beneath him. Luka reached out and grabbed the end. That false security, irresistible.

"Thom, no," Jena said. "It—"

"The other day . . . she was so angry. I told her I was sorry, that I didn't mean anything by it. But she said it didn't matter. She said if judgment comes—"

*. . . it will be from the mountain.*

The words were a roar in Jena's mind.

It was two short days ago, but felt like an age. The girl who had said that was someone she no longer recognized.

As she thought back to seeing Thom at the Source, something came to her with a confused kind of clarity. A boy must not be in the mountain. As children, it was one of the first things they learned. When the Seven crawled from the rock, the message had been clear.

As clear as the message Min's death had brought them?

Generations from now, might their own great-grandchildren learn at their mamas' knees about the danger of ropes, tell stories of how the mountain had rumbled that day?

She called up across the rock, fighting to keep her voice steady. "It wasn't anyone's fault, Thom."

"Then what happened?"

"I don't know, Thom. She just . . . why don't you come down? We can talk more easily here and . . ."

*You won't be able to fall.* Her sentence went unfinished, but the thought echoed loudly. Standing here, she couldn't help but recall that tiny figure tumbling toward her.

But it was all right, because Thom was descending. He came slowly at first, and then picked up speed as he fell into a kind of rhythm. For all his slightness, he was strong, and there was a sureness to his movements as he edged down the rope, hand over hand.

When he reached the overhang, he hesitated before maneuvering awkwardly past. The rope swung a little, and his feet scrabbled against the stone as he tried to stabilize himself. Jena ducked as debris showered around her.

A short while later, Thom was beside them, his feet reaching for ground. Luka clapped an arm around his shoulder, his other hand maintaining a firm grip on the rope.

Jena's instinct was to head for the trees, to get clear of the rock and the rope and this place, but Luka was already leading Thom beneath the curve of the mountain, motioning to him to sit.

"I'm sorry." Thom slumped to the ground. "I just wanted to be where she was. To see what she saw when she . . . it's dumb." He reddened, sheepish. "I wasn't going inside. I swear."

"It doesn't matter," Jena said.

She wasn't sure herself what her words meant. That it didn't matter because Thom hadn't gone inside, or that it wouldn't have even if he did? Her own thoughts had become slippery things, ungraspable. It felt like she was splitting open, her world upending itself from the inside out.

Luka crouched next to Thom. The ground here was scattered with loose stones, as if the mountain were crumbling at its base. Luka's feet scuffed through them, leaving lines like freshly swept paths. "You should come back. Get some rest."

Thom ran the back of his hand across his nose, snuffling. "I can't sleep. I can't think straight for missing her. And for worrying. About winter. About Mama."

"It will be hard for her," Jena agreed. "For all of you. When my mama died, I—"

"I don't mean that," Thom said. "I heard her and Papa talking. She's going to try again."

"What do you mean? Try for what?"

"For a daughter." Luka spoke slowly, as if something were in the process of clicking into place. "Berta said something to Dyan before. I didn't realize they were talking about your mama."

"But Min said your mama was broken. How can she?"

Thom looked stricken. "She said it's our only chance. And the Mothers said if she was careful . . . that they could help her. That there might be a way."

"Thom, no." Something clenched inside Jena. The thought of brittle bones pushing and pushing. The force of a birthing. And even if she survived, even if she birthed a daughter, it would be next season. There was still this winter.

"They said they'll give us extra now. Two bags, I think. And Mama said . . ." Thom's voice dropped to a whisper. "She said even if things go wrong, at least we'll get through the winter. Ernst and Jann can take wives next season. They'll have their own allocations then, their own families to think of. It'll just be the five of us, or four, if Mama . . ."

Something fierce rose in Jena. It was not anger

exactly but a kind of conviction. "She can't birth again, Thom. You have to tell her not to."

"She won't listen to me. She doesn't even know I heard. And it's Papa too. They decided together. They're doing it for us. They think it's the only way."

"It is," Luka said. "Unless we find another one." He turned toward Jena, his eyes blazing. "You have to go inside. I'll cover for you. I'll—"

"No," Jena said quickly. "It's bigger than that. All of this . . . what's been happening with the mamas. I think we have to tell people."

"And say what?" Luka scoffed. "No one will take you seriously if you show them some scribbled names and say you smelled something strange."

"I know," Jena said grimly. "That's why I'm going to get proof. The bottle, and the ledgers. I'll talk to Mama Dietz . . . and maybe Thom's mama too."

She felt light-headed, a sudden rush of something tingling in her limbs. She put a hand on Thom's shoulder. "We'll explain later," she said. "Just . . . don't worry. We'll make sure you're all right."

She thought of Min's trusting face. It was too late to help her, but this was something she could do. For her family. And for others too.

She squatted alongside Thom, one hand still on his

shoulder, the other tracking lightly along the ground for balance. The stones here were mostly flattened and weathered, but there was a pile of fresh debris, the scattering of rubble Thom had dislodged on his way down.

Amid the scree, her fingers struck an odd-looking pebble. It was larger than the stones around it, about the size of a plump wickerberry. But it was the color that set it apart. In the pile of dull gray, it seemed almost to glow, a pale, luminous blue.

Mica?

The color was similar, but this was nothing like the harvest. It was not a flat chip but a smooth rounded stone. And even more oddly, it had a hole in it. She felt it before she saw it, her fingers tripping across the slight indentation in the surface.

She was about to pick it up when she hesitated. This wasn't a roller or a crumbler, something the mountain had shed willingly; it was only here because of Thom, because of a boy who had hauled himself up the rock on a forbidden rope and kicked wildly at its side.

By rights, she should return it; at the very least, leave it where it lay.

But it was cool beneath her touch, irresistible. And

it was just one stone, she told herself. What could it hurt, to move a single stone?

She scooped it from the rubble and held it up to the moonlight, peering closely. What she had felt was not a hole, but a tunnel of sorts—a thin passage running right through the center of the stone, end to end.

This wasn't just a stone. This was something that had been *made*—fashioned with skill and care.

Luka's eyes widened. "Where did you get that?"

"It was on the ground. I think it fell when Thom was coming down."

"From up there?"

Jena stared at the spot where Thom had scraped against the side of the mountain. And as she did, her body went cold. It was the same place Min had stopped, where she had leaned toward the mountain's face.

Thom's words returned to Jena. *To be where she was. To see what she saw.*

Perhaps it was this, rather than the overhang, that had given Min pause. That had startled her, making her fall.

Luka reached out and plucked the stone from Jena's fingers. He held it close to his face, turning it slowly.

"Remember how I told you Berta had a pendant

from the old times?" He dropped the stone back into her open hand. It rolled back and forth for a few seconds before coming to rest. "It looks like this."

"Like this? Are you sure?"

"It's not exactly the same. Hers isn't as smooth. But it's definitely mica. It has a hole like this too."

Jena couldn't resist the urge to pick it up again. Knowing what it was made it feel different; it seemed heavier in her hand, more substantial.

"Do you really think it's a pendant? It's so small." She held it between her thumb and forefinger, trying to imagine it strung around someone's neck.

"Maybe for a child?" Luka suggested.

"And it's been up there all this time, since . . . ?" The image was in front of her suddenly, of the earth heaving, swallowing everything in its path—houses splintered like matchsticks, people tossed like rag dolls, a blue stone snapped from a flimsy string and lodged in the mountain's flank. Lying there all these years, waiting to catch someone's eye.

Her hand closed over it, gripping it tightly. In the curve of her palm, it felt smooth and solid—something to hold on to, to never let go.

※

Lia is back there at first light. It is dark in the mountain, but some feeble rays filter through the narrow crack in the rock.

She did not want to come back here, to remember. That face, those eyes.

*It is not my fault,* she reminds herself. But when she closes her eyes, the girl is all she can see.

She did not want to come back here, but she has to find it.

She cannot believe she has lost this precious thing. Cannot believe she didn't notice until she was out of the mountain, almost home. That heart-sinking moment when she looked down and saw her wrist bare.

It is not the stone itself. They are cheap at the markets, and if you have the will, you might even fashion your own. The bluestone is easy enough to find; it lies in rich, open veins right there on the ground, as if the earth were making them a gift of it.

She could do that. She could pick some up, strike it and wait for it to burn itself out. Father would shape it for her, rolling it around a thin sliver of wood to make the hole through the center. And this time she would be careful; she would choose a stronger piece of string, make sure it did not fray or snap.

That must be what has happened, because it could

not have slipped off. She had tied it firmly so it fit her wrist exactly. So it would never let her go.

Because it was special. Because it was her first present, on her first birthday. And this is why it cannot be replaced. This is why a new one will never be the same.

It was not really her birthday, of course; no one knew when that was. Father used to call it her "found outside the mountain" day, to joke that the earth had made them a gift of her too.

It was a gift he and Mother accepted. They picked her up and took her in. Asked up and down the coastline, sent word around the island. And when no answer came back, they shook their heads in disbelief. What kind of person would give up such a lovely girl-child? There were people who did such things, they supposed.

But *they* would love her. She would have a life with them. And so they made that day her birthday. Near enough, they said. That's how tiny she was, how frail.

They were not sure she would survive. But she grew stronger quickly, and when a year had passed and she was so much a part of their family they could hardly remember a time without her, they marked the day—with a plump goat on the spit and a birthday doll. And with a smooth blue stone on a slender string.

That precious thing she has kept close all this time.

Lia holds her breath as she scans the tunnel. And then her eyes fall upon it.

The string is lying on the ground beneath the crack in the rock. It is no longer a circle but a line, its two ends severed cleanly.

Her hand, she thinks, the way it scraped across the stone.

She swings her lamp along the ground. She does so more slowly than she needs because she doesn't want to reach the end of the tunnel. The end that will tell her what she already knows.

The stone is not in here. It is outside, and that means it could be anywhere. On the ground somewhere or on the side of the mountain. It hardly matters. People say the island is small, but for a girl seeking a single stone, it is impossibly large.

*It is gone,* she tells herself. She picks up the string and closes her fingers around it. It is so thin, so light, she might be holding nothing at all.

# CHAPTER 19

In the days that followed, the stone sat deep in Jena's pocket. Her fingers returned to it constantly, curling around it as if seeking comfort . . . or something else.

What did it mean that this had tumbled loose from the mountain?

There was no message in it, she told herself, at least not the way the Mothers would have thought. But still, there might be some meaning. Perhaps these were not, after all, the same thing.

Time passed slowly, seeming to thicken around her. Snow had begun to settle high upon the mountain, and with it, the advent of winter pressed close upon the village. Clouds hung, sluggish, in the sky above; it was as if the weather were holding its breath.

Every day, she led the line into the mountain, leaving the village at dawn. The first few mornings, Kari woke too. She sat up, rubbing sleep from her eyes, and wished Jena well. Kari was busying herself at the Center, helping Irina prepare for the winter. She was there until late at night, feeding and measuring and laying in stores.

She must be tired, Jena thought. For soon enough Kari stopped waking; when Jena rose, she stirred only slightly before rolling over and sinking back to sleep.

A distance had grown between them, and Jena longed to close it. There were times when she was on the verge of telling Kari what she had discovered, but she held herself back. She knew Kari was still uneasy about what had happened that day at the Center; her eyes lingered often on Jena, a hint of worry at their edges.

Before she told anyone else, she must have proof. But while it was all she could think of, there was no chance to return to the room where the ledgers were kept. With the season drawing to a close, the Stores had become a hub of activity that continued late into the night. Mothers bustled in and out, shoveling grain and beans into bags; others leafed through pages of names and numbers, brows furrowed. There was no telling when they would be there, when it might be safe to trip the lock and try again.

A week after she had talked Thom down from the rock, Jena led the line back from the mountain. Not from the harvest, for there had been none. There had not been a harvest since the new girls had started, since they had begun going in without ropes. The Mothers were uneasy, and the villagers too. Until the bags were distributed at Wintering, no one would know exactly how much their household would receive, but a week without a harvest was a long time. When Jena laid their empty pouches in front of Berta, the Mother would seek an explanation. Perhaps they had not yet done enough? Perhaps there was more they must do for the mountain to return them to its favor?

They were halfway across the Square when the noise began. Someone was yelling—a single voice at first and then others joining in. She heard footsteps scuffling and doors opening as people emerged from the buildings around her, drawn by the commotion.

A figure appeared around the corner, coming from the direction of the fields. It was a young boy, his face alight with glee. "I caught it!" he panted. "It was right there. I mean, not *right* there. I had to chase it. It tried to get away, but I caught it."

He had slung the bird across his chest, in the way of a hunter. A boy might watch a hunter, Jena supposed dully, as a girl might watch the line. The bird's neck hung limp against him. "I twisted it," he said proudly. "See?" He pulled the rope from his shoulder and held the bird out, an offering to no one in particular, or to everyone.

As he did, Jena saw the edge of one wing, slightly folded.

The bird had felt no pain, she told herself. But the thought was not enough to keep her knees from shaking. She stared at her hands as if some echo of the creature might linger there.

The boy moved past and with him the crowd that had gathered. The bird's head lolled from his hands, seeming to fix Jena with one unblinking eye.

"It mustn't have been strong enough."

Luka's voice was soft behind her. She didn't reply. Her tongue felt heavy in her mouth, her voice a shifty thing, unreliable. She couldn't trust it not to crack.

"We tried," Luka said. "It was just too weak."

He was right, but it was no consolation at all.

※

That evening, she hurried to the Stores, her key clutched in one hand. Her heart pounded, a caged thing beating wildly in her chest.

It was not yet late, and there were still people out. Behind the Stores men added bundles of firewood to the pile, and nearby a group of women sat shelling peas. From the open doors of the bakery, the smell of fresh-baked bread wafted, tantalizing.

There were no Mothers about, though. They would be gathered around the long table in Berta's kitchen, waiting for Jena. This afternoon, Jena had asked to meet with them. She said it was as Berta suspected—if they were to find favor with the mountain once more, there were things they must discuss.

She did not know how long she would have, but prayed it would be enough.

She slid her key into the lock and shouldered her way into the front room, taking care to lock the door behind her. Moments later, she was in the musty room down the hall. The bottle was where she had left it; she retrieved it from the shelf and tucked it into her satchel. But the ledgers were not so simple. Although a few still stood on the shelf, others lay scattered around the room. With Wintering drawing near, they must be in more regular use, and there was no easy way to identify the volume she had found her name in earlier.

She scanned the covers, hoping something familiar might strike her. If only she had thought to mark that particular ledger. She could hardly take them all; while one might slot unobtrusively under her arm, half a dozen clutched to her chest would be sure to attract attention. She flicked through the coarse pages of the closest book. This was a record of remedies rather than people, a recipe book of sorts. She set it aside and turned to the next. This one had names, but the pages were not organized into columns as the other ledger had been. She clapped it shut. There was a volume on the other side of the table, and she leaned across to retrieve it. She was sliding it over when a sudden sound made her freeze. A key was turning in the front door.

There was a creaking noise as the door swung open down the hall. Jena ducked low to the floor by the corner of the table. It was too late to make a run for the front room, too late to pretend she was here for the tunneling gear. She could only hope that whoever it was headed for the mica room rather than this one.

But the footsteps stopped just outside. The door rattled softly as a key slipped into the lock, then swung open.

Her thoughts raced. Perhaps she might say she was seeking a tonic—something for Mama Dietz or Ailin.

She had been in the front room, had seen the door ajar and thought someone was still here.

But then she ought not to be cowering here, hiding. She ought to stand, to say *Oh! I was looking for you.*

As the cloaked figure entered the room, she pulled herself upright. "Oh! I . . ."

The figure stumbled backward. The hood was drawn up, the face beneath it wide-eyed.

"Luka?"

He pushed the hood back and sagged against the table. "You gave me a fright."

"What are you doing here?"

He glanced at the ledgers. "The same as you, I guess. Berta said the Mothers were meeting, so I knew there'd be no one here." Berta's keys dangled from his fingers. "I thought I could put it back before the meeting finished. Aren't you supposed to be there?"

"Are they waiting for me?"

"They were talking. I heard your name mentioned, though."

"I should hurry." Jena turned back to the ledger.

"I can take it. You go. I'll hide it somewhere safe for later."

He reached for the book, but Jena motioned to him to wait. "I have to find the right one."

This one had columns, at least. And the notations looked similar. She turned the pages hastily, searching for *Dietz*. This might be the only chance she had before winter; she wanted to be certain.

Luka pulled some other ledgers from the shelf. "Do you want these?"

"I'm not sure. Wait a minute."

*Dietz* had been near the start, but she couldn't see it now. Maybe this wasn't the right book after all. There might be several like this, each with different families.

She jabbed a finger at Luka. "Pass that one."

As he handed her the book, something crossed his face. "That stone you found . . . do you have it?"

One hand went to her hip. "It's in my pocket."

"Can I see it again?"

She drew it out and set it alongside the ledgers, her fingers lingering briefly upon the cool surface.

Luka took it to the window. He held it aloft, trying to catch what little light filtered through from outside. "When I was getting the keys, I had another look at Berta's pendant. Remember I said hers wasn't as smooth? It's all chipped and worn, like it's older."

Jena continued flicking through the ledger. "I guess it is, then."

"They're both old. And this one's been in the mountain, so wouldn't it be worse?" Luka closed one eye and squinted at the stone. "But it's different too. That's what I can't work out. This hole through the center is smooth, but Berta's is all bumpy on the inside, and there are cracks, as if it broke when they were making it."

Jena nodded distractedly. "You should get away from the window."

He came back to the center of the room and placed the stone on the table in front of her. "Look how shiny it is. This isn't from the old times. It's newer."

"Don't be foolish. No one would waste mica like that now."

"I know, but—"

"We can talk about it later." A note of impatience crept into Jena's voice. She scooped the stone back into her pocket and gestured toward the ledgers. "I have to do this, before I'm missed."

But all of a sudden it was too late for that. Because the dim light had moved, throwing a dark shadow across the table. Someone was standing in the doorway, someone who had come in softly without making a sound.

*Thom,* she thought, hope flaring briefly. Perhaps Luka had told him he was coming. Perhaps . . .

No.

There was no hood masking this face. The Mothers had no reason to hide themselves.

# CHAPTER 20

"To think my own grandson would take my keys! And that cloak. It hardly becomes you." Berta sighed heavily. "I feared this might happen. What happened to the girl was difficult, but you cannot take things into your own hands. They will have enough if they are careful. If the rock allows it."

Jena's thoughts reeled. Berta thought they were here for Thom—to get extra for his family.

"Give me the mica." Berta indicated Jena's satchel, then glanced at the cabinet. "And whatever else you have taken for them. No one need know but us."

Luka stepped between Jena and Berta. "She hasn't got anything. She wasn't . . . it was just me. She was in the front room. She's been trying to stop me."

Berta narrowed her eyes; her gaze rested on Jena, thoughtful.

*It could work,* Jena thought. She could say she had been checking something on the map before she came to the meeting. Berta would believe her. They would leave the room together, lock the door behind them. She would walk by Berta's side down the long street to where the rest of the Mothers waited, speak with them of the line and the harvest and the mountain.

Something in her knew she could not bear to make that walk. She put a hand on Luka's arm. "It's all right." She withdrew the bottle from the satchel and set it on the table in front of Berta. "What does *ripening* mean?"

Something flashed across Berta's face; it was just the slightest glimpse before she composed her features, but it was enough. It was like a mask slipping; no matter how quickly it was snapped back on, what lay beneath could not be unseen.

"My mama." Jena leaned forward, keeping the bottle within reach. Her hands pressed hard onto the rough wood of the table's surface. "The ledger said seven moons."

"Because that is when she birthed." Berta's small frame seemed to fill the room. "We keep a record. You know this, child."

"No." Jena had not meant to lower her voice, but it came out as a whisper, cracked and broken. "You made the baby come early. You . . ."

Berta was so close now; her eyes were right there, and they were kind. They had always been so. Yet there was something hard in them too. Flinty and cold, like dull gray stone in the light of a head lamp.

Jena seized the bottle and stumbled around the table. Now the table was between them and she had some time—to take a breath, to clear her head. To think on what came next.

The door was at her back, wide open. She lunged for the remaining ledgers and scooped them up clumsily, one hand still curled around the bottle. Then she turned and ran out into the hall. Footsteps pounded, heavy and loud. Her own.

In the front room, the ropes hung, idle, on their hooks. The sudden image of that thin line, trailing limply down the mountain's side.

And then outside—across the Square and down the street. Homeward. By the time Berta reached her, she would have had time to show them—Mama and Papa Dietz, Kari. She would have had time to explain. Not a lot, but a little. Enough.

Wasn't it Berta who had taught her this—that all

you needed was the smallest crack? As long as there was an opening, you could find a way in.

There was a chill in the air, and the wind had picked up. The ledgers shifted awkwardly in Jena's arms. As she rounded the corner onto her street, rain began to fall. It was light at first but gathered force swiftly, the first sluggish drops yielding to a downpour that seemed to hurl itself upon her.

One of the ledgers fell, hitting the ground with a dull thud. The spine split, splaying the pages flat. She gathered it up as best she could, but scraps of paper flaked off and were snatched away by the wind. She clutched the books to her more tightly. They were damp, the covers and edges of the pages wet with rain.

She stopped, thinking to tuck them beneath her shirt. But they were too large and too many. And she was almost there now, just a few houses standing between her and home. But even as she began to run again, she found herself slowing. For there was Kari's house and here was home, and for the first time in years she turned her head and looked squarely at the old lot.

*A skeleton house.* She did not shy from the words but let them sit in her mind. Papa hadn't known the things she did, but he had challenged the Mothers all the same. He too had set out on a moonlit journey through these streets.

It had been quiet that night but was not so now. There were voices behind her, calling, yelling.

*Child! Come back.*

Doors opened around her. People emerged, blinking.

*What's going on? Are you all right?*

The ledgers were heavy in her arms, sodden. The ink ran together in dark rivulets, blurring and dissolving. Voices whipped around her. The wind roared, pressing close—almost painful—in her ears.

Ahead, her own door opened. Papa Dietz stood framed against the faint inner glow of the lamp, his silhouette filling the doorway.

"Jena?"

But there was another voice now, one she could not possibly be hearing and yet was as loud and clear as if it were right there.

*Wake up, Jena. It's time to go.*

And now she was turning, stumbling across the old lot, away from their house to the village outskirts and on toward the forest.

*That bird.* The way it had found that space in the trees.

She slipped one arm free and reached into her pocket, her hand clenching around the stone. *This is not from the old times.* Luka's voice was in her ears, clear as a bell.

She ran, lifting her face—to the mountain, to the sky. A bird's tail, disappearing, up and up. That space between the trees.

*It had been there all along.*

The path through the forest, her feet crunching with every step. A fork in front of her—the wide, looping way that wound back to the village, the narrowing path that led on to the mountain.

This moment, to choose.

She stepped onto the path and then looked back. Berta's slight figure stood in the distance, poised at the edge of the forest. Her cloak fluttered around her, battered by the wind. And there must have been a lull then, the wind easing just long enough for Jena to hear her calling. "Child, stop! You cannot go inside."

In spite of herself, Jena nodded. The Mother was right. One girl was not a line. One girl was not anything. Could she really go in alone?

Her reply came almost as a surprise. As if she had not realized what she was thinking until she heard herself say it. And no sooner were the words on her lips than they were snatched away with the last of the waterlogged pages, swallowed into the throat of the wind.

"I'm not going inside. I'm going out."

✳

*Jena is five, but it doesn't matter. Papa says numbers are not important anymore, not where they are going.*

*In the forest, leaves flutter groundward, wet with night. There is one so cold she thinks perhaps it is a snowflake. But it is too early for that, and when she puts a hand to her cheek, it is already gone.*

*The village is behind and the mountain ahead. It curves high above into the quiet dark. The space in front of them is a patchwork of stone, one piled upon the next like the blocks she played with when she was little. When she was four. Building tower after tower just to tumble them down.*

*She has been here with the village, to see this place they call the Pass, to remember.*

*She doesn't really remember. No one does. But it is a different kind of remembering, Papa says. You tell yourself the story, make a picture in your mind. And then it is almost like you are seeing it, almost like you were truly there.*

*They are at the rocks, and this is where they must stop.*

*Because this is the edge of things and there can be no more going.*

*But Papa turns to her and there is something in his face, something tired and old, but alive too, a dying flicker becoming a flame.*

*He holds the tiny bundle out, saying,* Here.

*Jena has been good and quiet, and so she takes her sister, gathering in the fragile limbs Papa has let dangle loose.*

Silly Papa. *She folds the girl into herself, wrapping her snug and cozy against her chest.*

Look after your sister, *Papa says, and she knows how to do it.*

*Something pulses beneath her finger, rhythmic and regular.* The heart beating in the head, *Papa had said, guiding her fingers over the fragile skin.* You mustn't press. Just let it be.

*Thinking on it makes her feel strange, and so she moves her hand, sliding it farther around the baby's head. And turns her thoughts instead to the rock that is in front of and above and around them.*

*They are going on a journey, Papa said, but there is nowhere to go.*

*And now they are here and she is holding the baby with her tiny soft bones and Papa is striding forward — climbing, squeezing through, moving rocks.*

Papa, no!

*Does she say it, or is it simply that the thought is so loud, drumming inside her mind?*

*It is all wrong, this. The baby should be at the Center, wrapped tight. Jena should be at home, tucked in bed. And Papa down the hall by the fire, waiting for the last ember to die.*

*They should not be here, doing this.*

*But Papa works faster now, his fingers scrabbling at the stones. There is a frenzy to his movements as he lifts one after the other, then hurls them clear.*

Look after your sister.

*Jena steps to the side, flattening herself against a lee in the rock. She turns the baby inward so she is cradled between her body and the mountain.*

Jena. *Papa's voice is hushed. When he turns, there is an odd light in his eyes.* Through here, *he says.* Follow me.

*Then there are sounds. From behind them comes the thrum of running feet. Twigs snap, their sharp cracks piercing the stillness.*

*There is light in the forest, muted pinpricks growing larger. Flaming torches bob toward them. Faces blur into focus. Voices call urgently across the night.*

Darius! Come away!

*Those dark cloaks, their soft folds flapping like wings. Alongside them, a man runs swiftly in the shadows. A single voice rises above the others.* Stop, Darius! Don't be foolish.

*It is Uncle Dietz. Papa turns. His eyes slide past Jena to the forest, to the lights advancing through the trees.*

*They will go back now, she thinks. Uncle Dietz will talk quietly to Papa, and he will come away. They will go home to the village and sleep, night falling gently over them like a blanket.*

*But Papa's gaze locks on hers and there is fear in it, and something else too. He looks like he wants to go in every direction at once. Every direction and none.*

Run! *he says.*

*And then he does.*

# Chapter 21

The walls towered above Jena, the chaotic jumble of rock wedged inside.

The Pass, impassable. It was here that the path had brought her.

No. She caught the thought, reeled it back in. This was the path she had chosen. Where else could it have led, once her feet began to walk it?

*Papa.*

Had it been raining that night too? She could not remember. All she could see was his back, disappearing. His hand, beckoning.

In her arms, the baby was still and quiet. In her mind's eye, there was a broken girl, a limp-necked bird.

She shook her head. One was then, the other now.

But suddenly they were both now, both then, the

distance between collapsing as cleanly as if it had never been.

✳

*Papa is going, but she is standing still. He is going through the rock. He is a head and then a hand and then the rock has swallowed him.*

*He cannot be there, where he is. It is wrong for a papa to be inside the rock, and Jena cannot move her feet.*

*There are voices behind them. Behind her.*

Child! Come back. *Uncle Dietz is calling and the Mothers too. Dots of light flare into halos that frame their faces.*

*Papa is gone, but he is just around that corner. There — that narrow shelf the rock has made of itself. That he has made, by moving the rock.*

*It is wrong to do this. It is . . .*

Papa! Come back.

*A few steps and she can see him. Up ahead is all rock, and he is pulling and tearing and tumbling. He is squeezing and climbing.*

You can't go inside, Papa. You are not in the line.

*The line. She is five and that is one year closer. She is five and that is two years left.*

Just two, Papa. Wait.

214

*Light flashes on the rock. She turns around. Mother Berta is there and Mother Anya too.*

*They are in front and Papa is behind. And there is a sound — a low rumbling, like a storm rolling in from the distance. Growing louder, growing nearer.*

*Jena! Papa calls, and so she turns again. And now he is in front and the Mothers are behind and there seems no way of getting that straight in her head.*

*And she cannot try because something else is happening. If this is a storm, it is like none she has ever known. It is beneath her feet somehow and all around. The sound rolls through her as if it is carving a passage for itself. The walls sway and buckle. The rock reaches out, curving over and across her.*

*Papa's hands still. He sees.*

*Jena!*

*Rocks tumble around her. The baby is in her arms, and then she is gone.*

*Papa is there, reaching.* Take my hand. Take my hand.

*Showers of small stones, the roar of something larger.*

*They are going, but there is nowhere to go.*

*There is a light and a voice. Stones rain from above. Papa is hunchbacked, buckling, but still he calls her on. A white-hot pain slices her shoulder, making her gasp and stumble.*

*Hands are reaching, in front and behind. She turns, grasps one, lets it lead her away.*

＊

The Pass.

There were rocks beneath Jena's hands, her own fingers scrabbling now. It was the simplest thing to move a stone aside. The simplest and the most difficult.

She would not hurl them as Papa did. Would not let them tumble, uncared for, to the ground. She would lift one between her palms and move it from here to there.

And then the next. The one that followed.

Until finally, a finger-width crevice, the narrowest of openings. Her arm found a sliver of space, eased itself in.

She looked behind her, the briefest of glances. The Mothers were back there somewhere, faint specks of light in the distance.

And ahead? Not Papa. She knew this, but still. She turned to the mountain.

She was fourteen and she was going.

She was gone.

＊

Lia moves quickly through the rock. Outside, dawn is breaking. By the time she reaches the crack, she will have all the light she needs.

Why did she not think of this earlier? If she peers through, there may be something she can see—some landmark she recognizes that will tell her where her birthday stone fell.

To think of the stone falling is to think of the girl doing the same, and so she tries not to. Who is to say what happened, where she went? There has been no commotion in the village, no word of a pale-faced girl who has tumbled off the mountain.

The girl is fine, Lia tells herself. And when she finds her stone, it will be as if nothing ever happened. She will have unstitched that day as cleanly as Mother unpicks a tangle of thread and begins again.

It is the smallest sound that draws her left instead of right. This is not the way to where the stone fell, but it is only for a minute—to follow that scrabbling sound, to see whatever scuttler is creeping its way through the rock. Then she will double back, continue.

It will only take a minute.

# Chapter 22

Stone tore at Jena's skin. Her fingers scraped along the rock, clawing for ground. A slickness to them now; they must be bleeding, though there was no way to see. She had no head lamp, no light. This was utter, deepest black.

Everything about this place felt wrong, against nature. There was no passage here, no sense, however slight, of the mountain opening up to let her through. This was a kind of trespass, each movement a small theft.

*A wrong thing. A right thing.* That bird, climbing the air.

How long had it been—four hours, five? She was desperately thirsty. She licked her lips, felt only dust upon them. Her throat rasped.

She could not have said when things began to change. At first it was the slightest whiff of movement in the air. And then something different about the rock. The surface around her was smoother, more like a wall than a haphazard pile of stone. It began to recede slightly, and then more so, until at last her arm, extending, found nothing. There was an opening here, a space to crawl into.

She pulled herself inside it, grateful. If she could not drink, she could at least rest, sit for a time before pushing on through the dark. There was no going back.

✳

Lia presses a hand to the wall of the tunnel. There are boulders here, wedged one upon the other. It is from there that the noise has come—from inside them or behind or . . . below?

She leans in, angling the lamp she carries into the tight spaces between. And as she sets her weight against the stone, it moves—just barely, one edge of rock teetering upon another.

She shines the light into the crack and puts her eye to it, expecting solid stone. If she is lucky, she might glimpse that scuttler, living its secret, rockbound life.

Instead, she sees space. A pocket of air extending. She draws back, considers.

She has never been a girl to see a box without opening it. To leave a lid pressed firmly in place.

She will move only one stone, and that just a little. The finest margin, to widen the gap.

She feels the sound before she hears it—a low rumble, as if the mountain were stirring beneath her.

She jerks her hands back as stones shower around her. The boulder she was moving is gone, fallen into space. Others rain around it, rolling and tumbling off a ledge beyond the gap, which is widening and widening even as the tunnel around her collapses upon itself.

She dives for the gap, hurling herself through. There is no telling what lies in the dark beyond the circle of lamplight. How deep the hole, how far the fall. There is only this moment, suspended, waiting for impact.

# CHAPTER 23

*Rockfall.*

Jena barely had time to register the thought when there was a sickening thud nearby. Another. Something grazed her shoulder, a glancing blow that sent her reeling.

She buckled, hands thrown uselessly above her head. The crushing weight of the mountain upon her, the stone floor rising to meet her like a slap.

There was so much sky and all of it stone. The roof was down, and there was no roof, no floor. It was just rock, all around her, the weight of everything pressing. The earth slamming a fist into its palm, and her in between.

She tried to move, to grab hold of something, anything, but all of it was tumbling, and her arms, her legs, were as useless as sticks, crushed, crumpling.

Rocks broke, and the sound of their shattering was inside her bones.

There was nothing but rock and darkness and pain, lowering upon her with each breath. Time seemed to swell, each moment fat and slow.

*I am fourteen,* she thought. *And that is all I will ever be.*

The light, the dark, winking out.

✳

When Lia lands, the force is hard and blunt. The air is pushed from her lungs like she is a bellows, pumped.

She lies still, tentative, testing. This arm. That leg. Somewhere nearby, there is a faint glow. Her lamp lies among the rubble, tumbled clear.

She blinks. It is a cavern of some kind—not a large space but not small either. Fine dust drifts through the wan light, rising from the freshly fallen stones.

She rolls to one side, suppressing a groan. Inches her way toward the light across the bedlam of rock.

*One stone,* she thinks. To move one and find the mountain coming down around you.

*Unstable,* they said, and now she believes them.

✳

*Jena is five. Is she five?*

*Perhaps a birthday has slipped past. The world seems to have melted and blurred.*

*There might have been a birthday, a doll. Has she missed it? She has been sleeping; it feels like forever.*

*There is a room here. Four walls around her. A face lowering over her own.*

Papa? *Something pounds in her head. A sharp knot of pain throbs in one shoulder.*

It's all right, child.

*There is a woman here. It is not Mama, but her eyes are kind. A smile hovers at the corner of her mouth.*

Here. *She holds out a spoon.* This will help you sleep.

I have had a bad dream, *Jena thinks.* Papa was there, and the baby. And before that . . .

*Her mind reaches for something, but there is a face over her own, a warm hand on her shoulder. She tries to sit up but sinks back down.*

Here, child.

*A spoonful of something, soft in her mouth. The air blankets her, warm and feathery.*

*It was a bad dream; that's all.*

*She sleeps.*

# Chapter 24

Jena had thought she knew darkness, but this was something else.

This was a kind of night that had fallen, close and final as a grave.

Something pressed heavy upon her, and it was the whole world. She tried to move a finger, a toe, but could not. The mountain had taken her and held her fast.

*This is where I will lie.* The thought spread out before her, leaden and dull. Some passages did not allow for return. The Seven had known this; she would learn it now too.

It was an embrace, she told herself, the mountain folding her into its arms. Stroking, soothing. In time, the stone would settle around her. In the valley, the sun would rise and set; shadows would lengthen and contract with the seasons.

*Observe the loss; fly on.*

One day, a way might open—a way for another girl, yet to come. One day someone might harvest her bones, feel them light as ash in the palm of her hand.

*Sleep, child.*

The world was blurring. She was tired, so tired.

*I'm sorry, Papa.*

It was only a whisper. In her mind all these years and now here in the mountain's dead air. She imagined it traveling through the rock to the place where he lay.

But then, impossibly, there was another voice.

"Hello?" It was faint and tentative, as if it were coming from a great distance. Her own voice, inside her head. It must be.

But it was louder now, and closer. *Hello?* And alongside it, another sound: a scrabbling and scraping, the noise of rocks rolling and dragging across one another.

Being rolled, being dragged.

The world lifting from her chest, a slim shaft of air, and—yes—light.

That voice again, shaking. "Is someone under there?"

# Chapter 25

*Hello?*

There was a light in Jena's face, pale but blinding in its closeness.

The weight was gone, and she had never felt such relief. Her limbs pulsed painfully as blood rushed back in.

She was no longer trapped but could not move. Above her, a floating shape resolved. A face lowered toward her.

"Are you all right?"

It was a girl, the light lending her skin an eerie glow. Her eyes were hooded, one half of her face in shadow.

Jena blinked. There was something familiar about the girl, but she could not place it. Her mind raced with faces, names, trying each in turn, but none fit.

She tried to sit up but could find no strength in her body. As feeling returned, it brought only pain. Her body felt like it had been scraped raw; there was nowhere that did not throb or sting. Her head was too heavy for her neck; in the base of her skull, a shrill beat pulsed.

"A rockfall," she rasped. "I . . ."

Images from the last few days swam queasily in front of her. And with them, a single sentence.

*If judgment comes, it will be from the mountain.*

"I'm so sorry." The girl's dark face seemed to flush. "I only meant to move one, but then . . . I didn't know there was anyone here. How could I know?"

"You did it? But who—?" Jena's voice cracked, faltered. There was grit in her eyes and mouth. Each ragged breath scraped air across her parched throat.

"Here." The girl set her lamp down and pulled at a strap across her chest, swinging a satchel around from behind her. She withdrew a flask from inside and twisted the lid free, then pressed the opening to Jena's lips.

The cool was instantly reviving. Jena let the water spill across her mouth. Some trickled down her throat; some ran along her chin and neck. She grasped the flask and began to tilt it, slowing the flow.

After a time, she pulled herself awkwardly onto her elbows and shuffled by slow, painful degrees into a sitting position. She passed the flask back. "Thanks."

It was a relief to hear her voice come out more cleanly this time, a certain steadiness returning.

"How did you get in here?" Jena asked. The girl must have followed her somehow, but it was strange because she was no tunneler. Though she was small enough, there was a fleshiness about her, as if she had not been properly wrapped. Her complexion was mottled in the way of a girl who spent her days in the fields; it seemed even darker than that, but Jena supposed that was the light.

At her words, the girl gestured vaguely at the wall of the cavern.

Jena twisted around but could not make anything out in the shadowy dark. "Did the Mothers send you?"

"Who? I don't . . ." The girl trailed off, an odd look on her face. She leaned toward Jena. "What's that?"

The stone must have fallen from Jena's pocket; it lay beside her on the floor of the cave.

The girl reached out, a kind of hunger in her eyes. Her fingers scrabbled in the dirt, closing tight around the stone. "Where did you get this?"

"I . . . found it." It was as much as Jena could manage.

"Well, it's mine. I lost it." There was an edge in the girl's voice, as if she thought Jena might argue or take it back. When she did not, the girl's expression softened. Her eyes searched Jena's, suddenly thoughtful. "But you fell. I thought . . ." She uncurled her fingers from the stone, which sat snug in the palm of her hand. "No, it wasn't you. The other girl was—"

"What other girl?" But even as Jena asked, she knew. And now she took the girl in properly—the odd cut of her shirt, the strange fastenings at the collar, the wooden clasp that drew her hair back from her face.

They were like nothing Jena had ever seen. In the village, in the world.

*This is not from the old times.*

"Where are you from?" she whispered.

"Near the inlet." The girl's reply was matter-of-fact. "On the east side, past the mill. How about you?"

"I . . ." A lump rose in Jena's throat; she could not seem to push words past it.

"Wait . . . you're not from Shorehaven, are you? White Bay, then? That other girl . . . her hair was like yours. I thought she looked strange. . . ."

Her voice faded into the background as Jena's

thoughts became louder. There was only one thing that mattered in what the girl said; once she had heard it, there was nothing else.

This was a girl from elsewhere, from outside. From a place—an idea—she had hardly dared believe in, even as she was heading there. And more than that—there were people out there, and villages.

The walls of the cavern seemed to swim around Jena. It is one thing to imagine, to believe something, and another altogether to see it with your own eyes. She pointed at the stone. "This is really yours?"

"It's my best bluestone. I've had it forever, since my first birthday." The girl hesitated. "Not that it was really a *birth*day. Father calls it my 'found outside the mountain' day, but . . ."

"How did you get in here?" Jena clutched at the girl's hand. "Do you know the way out?"

"Out? Of course." She turned and flashed her light on the wall behind her, then gasped. It was as if a river of rock had gushed into the cavern, a pile of boulders tumbled one upon the other. She stood up and picked her way across the rubble. Jena struggled to her feet and followed gingerly, pain sluicing through her with each footstep.

The way was blocked; any opening there had once

been was gone, hidden behind a wall of unsteady rock. The girl placed a hand on the pile of stones, then a foot. Immediately, there was a rumble from within, something shifting beneath, out of sight.

"Stop!" Jena's voice echoed off the walls. "You'll make it worse."

But how could it be worse? There had been a way, and it was gone. She stared at the jumble of stone. "How did you . . . ? Did you climb down?"

"Not exactly. I sort of . . . dived." The girl rubbed her arm ruefully, the corners of her mouth turning up in a lopsided grin.

The girl was not without her own cuts and bruises, Jena realized. Though it was nothing like you would expect for someone who had fallen—or dived—from such a height. "You must be broken," she said. "Let me see."

"Broken?" The girl batted at her arm like she was dusting something off. "I'm okay. Just a few bruises." She took a step back into the center of the cavern. "I guess we'll have to go your way." Her face creased in puzzlement as she scanned the stone walls.

Jena indicated the crack through which she had come.

"There?" The girl picked her way over to the

crevice. "You really came through here? I guess you'd better lead the way."

"It's too narrow. You won't get through."

"You did."

"That's different. I'm used to it. I'm . . ." Jena checked herself. The line would mean nothing to the girl; to speak of it would only invite questions Jena had no energy to answer just now. "I'm in here all the time," she finished.

"Me too," the girl said. "Besides, how else am I supposed to get out?"

She was right, of course. But it was more than that. With the ledgers lost, Jena had no proof of anything. There might be no way now to convince people of what the Mothers had done. But if there was an outside, a place where people turned mica into jewelry, then they would have no reason to tunnel or harvest or—Jena could hardly bring herself to think the word—*ripen*.

The girl had to come with her. If Jena returned to the village alone, who would believe her—Luka? Thom? No one who would be able to move rocks, to help clear a passage back to the girl. People would simply shake their heads and say she was mad after all. *Her papa's daughter.* What could you expect?

"I can do it." The girl was edging into the crevice, the whole of one arm now disappeared from view. The side of her face was pressed hard against the rock, and there was something in it Jena recognized. Something that made her approach and place a hand on the girl's other arm. "Not like that. Here."

The girl stepped back, and Jena slipped her own arm inside, showing her how to rotate her shoulder, work the angle. "See? You have to turn there or you won't be flat enough."

"I think I can do that. I'll try."

"Stay close. Watch me and do what I do." Jena slung the flask around her neck. "I'll carry this. And you'd better give me the lamp."

The girl handed it over wordlessly. It was an odd-looking device: rather than a chip of mica, it had a naked flame, muted behind a clear housing. There was a strange smell to it—some kind of oil, Jena supposed, like the larger torches they used in the village.

She turned to the rock. Then she stopped and looked back over her shoulder. "What's your name?"

The answer came quickly. "I'm Lia."

"Lia. I'm Jena." She eased herself into the stone. "Follow me."

# Chapter 26

Their progress was slow, but no slower than Jena had expected.

In some ways it was even a little faster. Because the girl—Lia—was fast. There were tricky corners where Jena had to wait, to turn back and position the light just so, talk her quietly through each movement: *Here, then there—see?* But as they went on, these became fewer. She would turn after a tight section to see Lia coming through unaided, a smile on her face, paying no heed to the fresh cuts and grazes that scored her skin.

At first, Jena wondered if she had been mistaken about the space. Perhaps the strangeness of her journey in had made it seem more difficult than it was. But it was not that. It was Lia herself. The girl learned quickly, almost as if the facility had been within her all along, waiting for a chance to reveal itself.

She had no reverence for the rock, though—that much was clear. She kept up a stream of chatter as they moved through, and Jena resisted the urge to hush her. This was not the line, not the harvest.

"What's it like where you live?" Lia twisted herself around a bend. "Is it like Shorehaven? I mean, I know you probably haven't been there. I haven't been to White Bay either. But Father told me things."

"It's just a village," Jena replied. "Like . . ."

*Yours,* she had been going to say, but even thinking it felt foolish. There was no reason to think the girl's village was anything like hers. The color of her skin, the flesh on her bones. The way she exclaimed as she made her way through the rock, as though it were a game, an adventure.

"I can't believe I'll get to see it." Lia exhaled loudly as the rock opened out around her. "How long do you think it will take? How long did it take you to get in?"

"I don't know," Jena replied distractedly. "I—"

"Maybe we could make a way through!" Lia burst out, then flushed. "Well, I kind of did, didn't I? Then wrecked it. But maybe we could do it again. Even just for you and me. We could meet in the middle and . . .

do things. I don't know. I just like it in here." She glanced at Jena, thoughtful. "What were you doing here, anyway?"

Jena twisted the lid from the flask and took a sip of water, then passed it to Lia. "My village," she began tentatively. "It's not what you think."

Lia wiped a hand across her mouth. "What do you mean?"

"I'm not from Shorehaven. Or White Bay."

"But there aren't any other villages." Lia frowned. "Where is it, then? What's it called?"

"It isn't called anything. It doesn't have a name."

There was a peal of laughter. "That's silly. Everything has a name."

Jena felt suddenly weary. It had never seemed odd before. Home had simply been the village, the valley, the mountain. What use was a name when there was just this one place and nothing to set it against? But now she wished she had a word she could give Lia, something that could speak for everything the village was and had been.

"Oh." Lia reached a hand to Jena's forehead. "You've got a bump there. No wonder you're a bit fuzzy. We can rest if you want."

"But I'm not . . ." Jena stopped. It would be easier

this way. Rather than trying to explain, to wait until they got there and let the girl see for herself. "I don't need to rest," she said. "We should keep going."

In truth, she needed to rest more than anything she could remember needing. Every muscle, every movement begged her to stop. To lie still for a while, to close her eyes.

She pressed a thumb against the lump on her head. Pain shot through her like a knife edge, sharpening her dulling senses. *Wake up. It's time to go.*

It was several hours before the valley's familiar smells began to filter through the rock. They were close now, but it was tight here and each small movement was hard won. For a time they had been upright, edging sideways through a slender crevice, but before long the space had tapered to a fine point, forcing them onto their bellies. They were the finest thread, slipping through the eye of a needle.

Another few minutes would do it, she thought. And it could scarcely come soon enough. Behind her, the girl's breath was shallow and fast, and though they had drunk sparingly, the flask was almost empty.

But it was odd, for surely this was the final bend. The leafy damp of the forest seemed to fill the air, as though it were almost upon them, or they upon it. And this jagged edge here—didn't she remember that too? The skin on one arm had torn as she pulled herself past it—no care in her then, only haste.

But if she was right, there should be light here. Or at least the darkness ought to have eased. Even if it was nighttime, there were always fingers of moonlight that filtered through by degrees. The opening should be visible up ahead. She pictured the stones she had moved aside, lying one neatly upon the other, waiting.

"Are we nearly there?"

It was the first such question Lia had asked, and Jena could hear the plea in it.

"Not long now," she replied. For everything in her said it was true and she must trust her instinct. And as she maneuvered herself around the turn, she saw it—the shape of something emerging from the gloom ahead. The space above opened out, the roof drawing up and away. This was the place she remembered—narrow but tall. The height of a girl and a little more besides.

"We're there," she said. "We . . ."

There was something wrong. The light was not as it should be. No clean sliver of it indicating the space through which they must pass, but rather slices of light at haphazard angles to each other, as if the opening had been cut into tiny, impossible pieces.

She blinked. The shapes resolved into clearer focus. And as they did, she froze.

The opening was stoppered with stones. And this was no rockfall. There was nothing haphazard about the way the stones lay—they were wedged tightly, jammed in place.

The Mothers had sealed them in.

Jena felt suddenly faint. The ache in her head shrilled to a fine point, her vision clouding. She stumbled as she tried to stand, and had to grab at the rock to keep from falling.

"What's wrong?" Lia's voice was a whisper.

Jena could find no words to reply. The Mothers' faces crowded through her mind—Anya's hand in hers, guiding her through a corner of the maze; Irina, checking her wrappings, her touch firm but gentle; Dyan pressing a healing poultice upon a wound, brow furrowed with concern. And Berta, all these years, always there, always everywhere.

She straightened, willing her thoughts to clear.

"Wait." She ran a hand along the wall in front of her. These were not the stones she had moved. They were larger, heavier. She pressed upon the nearest one with all the strength she could muster, but it did not budge.

Her fingers probed for crevices, tracking slowly upward. She was almost at full stretch when she felt it—a notch of space in the very top corner, where the pile met the smooth face of the mountain.

She flattened herself against the wall and beckoned to Lia. "Here." She passed her the lamp and flask and began to climb, pulling herself awkwardly up the column of stone.

The gap was a head's width, no more. But the outside was right there and this was the way. Must be, for there was no other. She threaded her fingers through and then her arm, rotating her elbow and then her shoulder. The head's hard plates, stubbornly solid. She flattened one ear to the rock, felt it scrape as she passed through. A thin trickle of blood slid down the side of her face.

Her hands found purchase on the rock outside and steadied. She was high enough that an uncontrolled fall might break her; she could not let that happen now, after everything.

Another rotation—the hips; another scrape. A tear? She would not reach down to find out. Because she was through now, her feet kicking clear, swinging out and down the face of the pile, finding footholds.

A few seconds later, a hand appeared; Lia's arm protruded to the shoulder. She pressed her face to the crack. "My head," she said. "How did you . . .?"

"You have to rotate," Jena said.

"It's too tight."

"There's a way. You have to find it."

Lia's arm tensed, her hand clenching into a fist. There was a scuffling sound, an exclamation. Then her fingers uncurled and her arm flopped down, hanging loosely over the rock. "You'll have to make it wider."

"I can't." Jena's reply was swift. She had taken the measure of things at a glance. There was no way she could move these stones by herself. She squeezed Lia's hand. "I'll get help."

"You're going?" Lia's voice quivered like a bowstring that has just loosed an arrow.

"I have to. I won't be long."

"But I can't stay here alone. I . . ." Lia trailed off. "All right." There was a sudden firmness in her voice, a decision. She pulled her hand free and began climbing down the inside of the wall.

"I won't be long," Jena repeated. "I promise."

As she clambered down and scrambled into the forest, she could only hope she was right.

# Chapter 27

She was on the outskirts of the village when she heard the sound: a single voice rising into the night, shrill and urgent.

The village was dark. It was early evening, but no lamps shone in windows; no warm squares of orange flickered a welcome. It was as if the place had been stripped of life, hollowed out.

Though the moon was full, it was shrouded in cloud, dim and distant, the faintest echo of light. But above the Square a blue glow blurred the night's edges. It was from here that the sound came, and Jena hastened toward it. She had planned to steal quietly through the streets, to find Luka and Thom and hurry back to where Lia waited, but that was impossible now. For the glow could mean only one thing—the Mothers had gathered the village for the Wintering allocation. She would not find Luka and Thom at home or helping out with the wood or the stores; they would be in the Square with everyone else, waiting for their name to be called, for their turn to step forward, arms outstretched.

*Thanks be. We gratefully receive it.*

But instead of that soft murmur, there was another sound. It was low at first but seemed to gain intensity as she approached. As she reached the final corner, she could feel it—the sense of something building. And above it, that voice again, calling. A voice she did not know well but recognized with a shock all the same.

Thom stood in the center of the Square, shouting and straining toward the table where the bags of mica lay. The Mothers blocked his way in a ragged but unbroken line. Though the night was dark, bracketed lamps on the nearby wall lit the area near the table, lending the front of the gathering a feeble light.

Thom's brothers jostled around him, grabbing for a hold as he twisted and turned, somehow managing to keep himself just clear. Through the melee of flailing limbs, Jena caught a glimpse of his mama's pale features. Her lips were moving—quickly, ceaselessly, as if she were trying to talk him down, to soothe him in the way you might a child who has been swept up in a fit of temper.

Jena crouched low in the shadows on the bakery veranda. From her vantage point against the wall, she scanned the crowd for Luka but could not spot him in the throng of people. In any case, there was nothing she could do now. She could not show herself without Lia by her side. She would have to wait until the gathering dispersed and she could get Luka alone.

She turned, hoping to slip off the veranda and get more distance from the crowd. But as she straightened, she found a face staring directly into hers. Renae was inside the bakery, looking out. Her eyes widened. "Jena?"

Before Jena could put a finger to her lips, Renae had rushed through the door. "Thanks be!"

"Renae, no . . ."

But it was too late, for heads were turning. Someone broke away from the rear of the crowd. Murmured something, causing others to follow. And then Renae called out, her cries mingling with Thom's. "It's Jena! She's all right! She's here!" Her arm was on Jena's shoulder, urging her off the veranda and into the crowd. Gasps punctuated the air around them.

"Jena?" There was a hand on her arm, a hoarse voice in her ear. Before she could speak, she was swept into a hug, familiar arms reaching for her as they had so many times across the space between them. "But how are you here? What happened?" Tears glistened in the corners of Kari's eyes. "The Mothers said you went in alone and—"

"But you're dead!"

A deep voice echoed across the clamor. Jena turned. It was one of Thom's older brothers, a tall, ruddy-skinned boy who shared none of his ghostly features.

"Dead?" Jena's breath hitched in her throat. Her gaze locked onto Berta's across the crowd. There was something in the Mother's face she could not read. Fear? Relief? Sadness? Surely it could not be all of these at the same time.

"Child." Berta's voice was low and gentle. "Thanks be. We thought the mountain had taken you."

"Is that why you sealed me in?" Jena had lowered her voice to match Berta's, but now she raised it again, speaking out into the crowd. "They blocked the opening. They—"

"It was us." It was another of Thom's brothers who spoke. He glanced around him at the others. None of them would meet Jena's eyes. "They asked us to. They said—"

"I could have died," Jena said.

"We thought you had." Berta held her hands out, palms upturned as though she were making an offering. "That the mountain had chosen you . . . to be with your papa, your sister. We meant only to seal the Pass, so such a thing could not happen again. And to give you stones, to mark your passing."

"To honor you," Mother Dyan said.

"To *honor* me?"

"We meant no harm," Berta said quickly. Then she hesitated, something in her face faltering. "You must believe me, child. We never meant to—"

"It is not we who decide." Dyan held up a hand, cutting her off. "It is the rock. In this, as in all things."

"Jena," Berta began again. "I . . ."

The air between them seemed suddenly heavy. Then Dyan continued. "The mountain has released her," she said. "It is a day." At her words, the crowd began to chant again. *Thanks be. It is a day.*

Someone tugged on Jena's sleeve. "Did you find a harvest, child?"

"A harvest?" Jena felt like she had been jolted from dreaming. "No, I . . ." She trailed off. Thom stood in front of her, and the Mothers too. The table with its precious mica. All thoughts upon it, hungry, hoping.

*You must believe me,* Berta had said. But there was no *must* anymore, no weight to her words.

Jena stepped into the space and turned to face the crowd. The night stilled around her. She gestured at the bags that lined the table.

"We don't need this." She was the only sound, her voice a feeble thing struggling to find a hold. From the far side of the Square, Papa Dietz threaded his way toward her; Mama Dietz was at his side, with Ailin in her arms. "There's an outside," Jena said. "We can go there."

Gasps and exclamations rose from those in the front. Others turned to their neighbors. *What did she say?*

"There's an outside," she repeated, more loudly this time. She tried to speak as she once had to the line. *Let's go. This is the way.* No matter what she was saying, the message was always the same. *Trust me. I speak truth.* "There are people out there. Villages."

Mother Vera held up a hand. "And you've seen this, child?"

"Not yet. Lia told me. She's—"

"Lia?"

"She's a girl from outside. She . . ."

Even as the words came from her lips, she was

dismayed at how foolish they sounded, like a story a child might dream up.

"And where is this girl?"

"She's inside still. At the Pass."

"Where you went in," Vera said softly. "As your papa did once." She reached a hand to Jena's head. "You're injured, child. You must let us take care of you."

Jena stepped back. "I'm all right. We have to get Lia. She's waiting."

Dyan was beside her then. "Child, you have been under a great strain. To follow your papa's path into the mountain . . . to conjure a story like this. You must rest. I have something that will help."

One hand reached for Jena, and the other disappeared into the folds of her cloak.

"Poor thing," someone said. "She's not in her right mind."

Dyan's hand emerged, a bottle clutched between her fingers.

"No. We have to get Lia out. We . . ."

The night seemed to sway; stars swooped toward her, blinding. How long had it been since she left the girl? Already their journey through the rock had taken on the blurred quality of a dream.

"You have to believe me," she said. "We don't need to tunnel anymore. We don't need a line or . . ."

"Jena." Mama Dietz was in front of her, and without meaning to, Jena found herself reaching, scooping Ailin into her arms. She clutched the baby to her chest and hurried away—from the throng of people, from the Mothers. To a space where she stood alone, where even those close by stepped quickly back.

"We don't need wrapping. We don't need *ripening*." Her hands worked at the thin blanket around the baby, and then the wrappings. The skin beneath was soft and warm.

"Ripening?"

"What is she talking about?"

"What is she *doing*?"

Ailin began to wail, a shrill, spiraling cry. Her tiny arms flailed as if fighting the very air around her.

"Come, child. You must be so tired."

"You need to rest."

Jena stumbled back as the Mothers approached. Then she felt someone at her side. "Here, let me take her." Kari's voice was low and gentle.

Jena hesitated. This weight in her arms, so light and yet so heavy. *Look after your sister.*

And then something caught her eye—a shadowy

figure behind the table, something familiar in its movement.

Luka? But there was someone else too, a smaller figure following him tentatively. A faint pinprick of light moved with them — a fading lamp on the verge of extinction.

But still — a flame. A weary hand setting it down upon the table, unthinking, unknowing.

A spark flared. Slow and stealthy at first, then roaring suddenly to life. Blue light exploded, filling the square, everything awash with it.

The mica was on fire.

# Chapter 28

People threw their arms up, staggered back.

Though Jena was not close, she instinctively swung away, shielding Ailin from the flaring force of the heat.

"Water!" Someone darted forward, cup in hand. A thin stream of liquid arced briefly through the air, then trickled uselessly to the ground. The last dregs of a drink, perhaps? It was too little by far.

A few people peeled from the crowd and raced for the well. But others stood rigid, as if the flames had fixed them in place. Then a figure ran toward the table, shrugging off her cloak as she ran, stretching it in front of her like a blanket.

Through the flames, Jena saw Luka's eyes widen. "No!" He made to reach for her, but the table—the fire—was between them. And it was too late now, too late to stop her.

Berta was upon the fire and it was upon her. She gave a terrible scream as she flattened herself against the burning table, the cloak beneath her, blanketing, smothering. The flames dipped, waned, then began to lick tentatively upward once more from the hem of her cloak.

Berta did not scream again but moaned, a low guttural sound. Her body continued to press upon the cloak. She arched her neck, a wild, animal look in her eyes.

Luka careered around the edge of the flames. He lunged for Berta, one hand raised high to shield his face, the other latching on to her leg. He pulled desperately at her. "Help her! Somebody!"

It was as if a spell had been broken. People surged to the table and began beating against the flames with coats and aprons. They returned from the well with pitchers and pots and threw the contents onto the fire. Others moved in and flanked Berta, helping her up.

The old Mother's face was twisted with pain. Something was dripping from her hands. *Water,* Jena thought, but no droplets hit the ground. As the

Mothers led Berta away, liquid hung from her fingers in an unmoving stream. Not water, but her own skin. Jena fought back the nausea that rose in her throat.

Behind her, where the mica had been, was little more than smoldering cinders.

"The harvest!" There were cries from the crowd. Some people sank to their knees in the dirt. But others were fixed on Luka; he was staring after Berta, pain etched into his face.

"It was him," someone called. "I saw it."

A low rumble rippled through the gathering. People began to press toward Luka.

But then a small voice came from behind him. "It was my fault. I didn't know there was bluestone in those bags. I'm sorry. I put the lamp down. I was just so tired. I—"

"Lia?" As Jena spoke, the crowd stilled, parting silently around her.

"Who is that?" Kari was beside Jena, her breath warm in her ear. "I don't . . ."

She didn't need to finish. Because above them the feathery clouds had torn one from the other, letting moonlight stream down upon the Square.

And as the pale beams bathed her dark skin, her curious clothing, Lia began to speak.

"My name's Lia. I'm from Shorehaven. From outside. I . . ." Her gaze searched the sea of faces before resting upon Jena. Then she looked out at the towering hands of the mountain, as though she could not take in what she was seeing. "I thought you were from White Bay. I thought you were just fuzzy from that knock on the head."

Jena stared from Lia to Luka. "But how . . . ?"

He held up his hands. They were raw and bloody, as if he had scraped them against something, as if . . .

"I went to look for you," he said. "But I found her instead."

Papa Dietz broke through the crowd. "I don't understand. The Mothers . . . they said you were gone. And now . . ." He glanced at Jena. "Is it really true?"

She nodded, her eyes fixed on his.

"And there's a way?"

"Not anymore. But we can make one." She gestured at the charred remains of the harvest. "We have to."

A question had been floating in the back of her mind, and now she allowed it to surface. "Papa . . . my papa . . . did he know about the outside?"

At her words, Papa Dietz seemed to crumple. He put his face in his hands, his shoulders heaving silently. When he looked up, his eyes were red. "He talked about it after your mama died, but there was nothing to it . . . nothing but grief and wishful thinking. I thought he would get past it. I never dreamed . . ." One hand had balled into a fist, and he uncurled it slowly, reaching out to rest it on Jena's shoulder. "To lose him like that . . . and your sister. I can't forgive myself for letting it happen."

"It wasn't your fault," Jena said. "Papa, he . . ."

She stopped, because something had changed in Papa Dietz's face. He was staring at Lia.

"Shorehaven," she was saying, in response to a question from the crowd. "And there's White Bay on the other side. That's where I thought Jena was from, but . . ." Her lips curved in that curious crooked smile. "Does this place really not have a name, then?"

Jena felt something inside her shift, a current stirring. Was it Papa's face or Lia's smile? Or was it simply that a crack had opened in her mind, letting her slip inside it?

*Everything has a name. A village. A girl. A six-moon baby hovering on the edge of life. A strong name, sealing you into stone. A light-as-air name, opening into sky.*

*Seren.*

*Lia.*

Not a birthday but a "found outside the mountain" day.

Jena blinked heavily, letting her eyes stay closed a beat longer than they needed. In her arms, Ailin was quiet and still, as if she too were holding her breath, waiting.

The crowd between them was a tunnel again, the past and present collapsed in a single, perfect moment.

*Do not fall, but if you must . . .*

"Jena?" Kari's arm was around her.

*Do not fall.*

"It's all right. I'm okay. It's just . . ."

In the pale light, she locked her eyes on Lia's, forcing into her voice a steadiness she could not imagine ever feeling again. "I think you're my sister."

# CHAPTER 29

"It's perfect." Jena pressed her shoulder against Lia's. It was so strange, but so right too—standing here in the dappled shade flanked by sisters.

"Thank you." Thom was on his knees in the damp grass by Min's grave. Lia's bluestone nestled in a hollow alongside the water stone their mama had laid.

Lia had told them what happened, and though it hurt to hear it again, it was good to know. To make what sense of it there was to be made. There were tears in Thom's eyes but the ghost of a smile on his lips. He seemed, if not happy exactly, then satisfied. Content.

He didn't blame Lia, he said. She could not have known.

Still, Lia was stricken with guilt. The gift of the bluestone did nothing to ease it, but it was something. And what stone could be more fitting for Min?

"I'm so sorry," Lia said again. "I wish I could have met her."

"She would have liked you." Thom rose and they stood together, looking down upon the grave.

*Thank you.*

Jena did not speak the words but let them remain a whisper in her mind. And this, she knew, was gratitude—not something that rolled easily off the tongue, but something wrenched from deep within.

In a curious way, it was Min who had saved Jena and Lia. When the Mothers offered Thom's brothers extra mica for sealing the Pass, they could scarcely refuse. But it was Thom who had insisted on placing the last stones at the very top, and in doing so had left a space—not so much that it would draw the eye from the ground, but large enough all the same.

It wasn't that he thought Jena was alive, he said. It was simply that he could not forget that moment when the earth had closed over Min. He didn't want to feel that again, couldn't bear to be part of it.

Jena sighed and looked out across the clearing. On the far side, a knot of villagers had gathered alongside the Mothers. Luka was on his knees in their midst, smoothing a last clod of earth over the freshly turned ground.

Berta had lingered two days after the fire, but in the end her burns were too severe. The Mothers said she had lacked the strength to heal, but Jena knew it was more than that. There was a brokenness to her. Jena had seen it when she stood by her bedside. How small she had seemed, swamped by a pile of heavy blankets, as though she were receding into herself.

Berta had not asked for forgiveness, said she knew she could not expect it. Her sunken eyes pleaded silently with Jena; she wished only for her to understand. That they had meant no harm, that their thoughts had been only for the line, for the survival of the village.

It was what the Mothers had countered when Jena told the villagers about the ripening, about the notes in the ledgers and the rubus.

*We did not know. We could never have imagined.*

Now, watching Luka kneeling in the dirt beside Berta's grave, it struck Jena that those were two utterly different things.

"Are you all right?" Kari put a hand on Jena's shoulder.

"I'm fine." Jena reached up and locked her fingers briefly with Kari's. Then she let go and began to walk across the clearing. When she was a few steps from him, Luka turned, seeming to sense her approach. He pressed a lingering hand against the earth, then rose to his feet. "Are you ready?"

She was. There was nothing here for her now. And she had no wish to stay and hear the Mothers repeat what they had said so often in the days following the fire: that even if there was an outside, that did not change the fact of Rockfall. The anger of the mountain, the salvation of the Seven. It was unnatural to carve a path through the stone. It was an abomination for a man to be inside the mountain. Judgment would surely come.

They had salvaged what little remained of the mica, repacking it into bags and taking up the ledgers anew. For those who remained faithful, there might yet be an allocation.

Jena scanned the faces of the villagers clustered around the Mothers; worry and fear were etched deep upon them. Though no one could argue with the fact of Lia, for some, the convictions of a lifetime were not so easily shed. Despite everything, this was something Jena understood.

But as the Mothers began to speak, Jena turned her back, letting their soothing tones fall away behind her. Luka drew alongside and they walked back to where the others waited.

As if in unspoken agreement, they looked up toward the mountain. You could not see the Pass from here, but they all knew what lay beyond the trees.

"All right," Jena said. "Let's go."

# CHAPTER 30

There was so much light.

Up ahead, Lia's silhouette was framed against sky.

An arm's length, perhaps two, and Jena might reach out and touch it.

And that smell, so thick now. It seemed to saturate the air, every breath drawing it deeper inside her.

When they had first smelled it, Jena thought it was gas. She dropped the tow rope on the trolley of rocks she and Lia were hauling and called to the others to clear the area. Papa Dietz and the other men let their pickaxes and shovels clatter to the ground and began to run back down the tunnel toward the distant light of the valley.

But Lia did not run. She stood perfectly still, a slow smile growing on her face. And when Jena shook her arm, urging her away, she said, "That's not gas. It's the ocean."

The others were still inside. The tunnel was not yet through, but they had opened this crevice. A crevice through which the smell of the ocean wafted. A crevice that was wide enough for a girl or two.

Lia edged across the opening, making room.

Jena hesitated. This moment of finding the light, leaving the mountain. When she would close her eyes, pull herself clear.

This moment she had lived so many times before, and yet none.

Eyes open this time. Let this new light come as it comes.

It came—bright, warm, enfolding.

"See?" There was pride in Lia's voice, as if she had made the world, as if she were a mama showing off a new daughter.

There was a blast of color. A green so vivid it made Jena blink. A burnished brown that seemed to ripple and sway. A thousand slender stalks ordered one way and then the other by the breeze.

Crops, at this time of year? Jena crawled to the lip of the opening, then set her back against the stone, her knees hugged close against her chest. Around them, patches of snow had settled here and there on the craggy rock face, but there was none on the ground below.

Had she ever felt sun like this? She was drenched in it. She leaned out a little, peeling herself from the mountain.

As her eyes adjusted to the light, another color resolved itself. Between the browns and greens were seams of blue. Outcrops of stone dotted the narrow strip of land below them, like fat knuckles that had punched up from underground, shot through with mica. With bluestone. As if the earth had turned itself inside out and said, *Here, take it.*

And beyond it was another blue, this one deeper, and not static but moving—rippling and curling as it flowed in to the edge of the land and then back again.

"Shorehaven is around there. You can't see it from here, but . . ." Lia indicated a long spur of rock that jutted out nearby and ran almost to the water.

The slope around them was overgrown, carpeted with vines and moss and small, scrubby bushes. They were still in the Pass, but it was clear that no rocks had fallen here for generations. No grief-crazed hands, scrabbling at stones, had made things tumble down anew. Anyone coming to it now would think it just another rugged crag on the stony face.

The crevice they had followed had angled steadily upward but had not strayed much to the left or right; they were somewhere above the line of the tunnel, Jena thought. It would emerge, when it did, almost directly below where they now sat.

"Should we go?" Lia motioned toward the ground.

The climb would be easy enough. Although they were high, the slope descended gradually, spilling out onto the plain in measured stages. Beneath them, the rocks of the Pass led away and down. If you looked at them a certain way, they were almost like steps.

Lia had begun to move forward when Jena put a hand on her shoulder. "Wait."

"What is it?"

"I . . . I wanted to say I'm sorry."

"For what?"

"For letting go of you. I was supposed to look after you. I was holding you and then . . ." Jena lowered her eyes. "I just let go."

Lia was silent for a while, thoughtful. Then she spoke. "It was good that you did."

"Good?"

"If you hadn't, I would have been in the valley with you all this time." Her face softened. "I mean . . . I would like to have had a sister. But then I'd never have lived outside. And I wouldn't have been in the mountain that day, with my weird hair and my funny clothes, waiting to become your proof."

Jena inhaled sharply. "But—"

"You did look after me. You looked after both of us. We just didn't know it till now." Lia flashed her crooked smile. "Come on." She turned once more and began to make her way down the slope, her movements nimble and quick.

As Jena watched her go, she felt something inside her ease. An old knot—one she had not realized was there—slowly loosening.

In a minute, she would go down the mountain, to the plain, to the village, to the sea.

In two days, the point of a pickax would open the smallest hole.

In three, a larger one. And they would begin to come through. Her people, her world, out here.

To Shorehaven or White Bay? Or to make their own place, give it a new name?

No matter, those things. For now, she closed her eyes, breathed deep, opened them again.

That light. That slim figure, clambering easily down the slope below.

And beyond Lia, in the distance, something else was moving. Out in the blue, a bird freewheeled, buoyed from beneath by an invisible updraft—no fear in it, no haste, wings spread wide, open to the sky.

# ACKNOWLEDGMENTS

For me, a story comes from many places. This book owes a large debt to Kafka, whose leopards set the idea in motion; a smaller one to C. S. Lewis, whose underground world of Bism shifted my eight-year-old thinking in fundamental ways; and many more to people and stories whose traces I haven't yet detected. I'm grateful to everyone who makes art and ideas and adds them to the well from which we all draw.

I also owe particular thanks to a few people. First, to the team at Walker Books Australia and especially my editor, Sue Whiting, who has an uncanny talent for helping me make my work the best version of itself it can be.

To Amanda Betts, who just gets it, and whose combination of steady calm and wild enthusiasm helped talk me out of the mountain when it felt tempting to stay inside.

And finally, to Carl and Bailey, for impromptu brainstorming sessions and assistance with character names, plot holes, and roadblocks of all kinds. For their patient tolerance of my many foibles and the fact that when they hear me shout, "I wrote a sentence!" they know me well enough to call back, "You deserve a reward!"